A FISTFUL OF DEMONS

A HANNAH HICKOK WITCHY MYSTERY BOOK TWO

LILY HARPER HART

HARPERHART PUBLICATIONS

ONE

"*H*owdy, pardner."

Hannah Hickok, her barmaid uniform putting her assets on full display, leaned over the partition in the saloon so she could flirt with Cooper Wyatt, the head of security at Casper Creek. Technically, Hannah wasn't a barmaid. Sure, she was playing one for the day, but she was actually the new owner of Casper Creek, a cosplay Western town set in Kentucky. She'd inherited the town from a grandmother she didn't know until the woman was already gone. Now she was settling into her new reality with as much energy as she could muster.

She was having more fun than she ever imagined.

Cooper, mirth filling his eyes, leaned back in his chair and gave her a long stare. "No one here says pardner," he said finally.

"I do ... and I'm here ... so that's not really true." Hannah's grin was so wide it threatened to swallow her entire face. "What are you doing?"

Cooper wasn't sure how to answer. In truth, he wasn't doing anything. He didn't want to admit that though, because then she might turn suspicious about why he was hanging around in the saloon in the middle of the afternoon when he should be working. In truth, he simply wanted to be around her... which was a humbling thought.

Before Hannah came to town, Cooper was happy with his life. He wasn't involved with anyone, a deliberate choice, and he opted to focus on his job. All of that fell by the wayside the minute Hannah showed up. As fond as Cooper was of Abigail Jenkins, the woman who took a chance on him after he returned from active service overseas, Cooper couldn't help being attracted to her granddaughter.

He hated himself for it, but that didn't stop him from flirting.

"I'm keeping Casper Creek safe," he teased, smirking when she rolled her eyes. "That's my job."

"Yeah, yeah, yeah." She glanced around the empty saloon and then skirted around the counter so she could slip onto the stool next to him. She looked to have something on her mind. "There's one more group coming through."

He nodded, unsure where she was going. "I know. They should be here at any moment. They'll hit the south side of the town before coming here, though."

"Yeah." Hannah cocked her head and rubbed her cheek. She appeared fidgety, which immediately put Cooper on edge.

"What's wrong?" He was legitimately worried. Hannah had only been in town for a little over two weeks. She'd settled in her grandmother's digs above the saloon relatively quickly — and with only minimal fanfare — and had quickly thrown herself at the business end of her inheritance. She'd never been in this particular position before, but she was gung-ho to learn. Her first week in town had been a busy one. A body dropped, evil witches from across the creek had made their presence known, and she'd found out she was magically inclined, something she swore she knew nothing about.

Since then, after the takedown of a murderous witch, she'd slipped into her role as town leader with little complaint. Honestly, Cooper was so impressed with her attitude he couldn't help but wonder how much of it was an act. He'd spent the last two weeks watching her for signs of a mental breakdown — it's not every day one finds out they're a witch with actual magic at their disposal, after all — but she'd held strong.

This was the first whiff he'd gotten that she might be uneasy.

"Why does something have to be wrong?" Hannah asked. "Why do you always jump to that conclusion?"

"Because I'm head of security and it's my job to keep the workers — and you — safe. You're acting like you need to tell me something I'm not going to like. I'm preparing myself for the worst so I can handle it."

"Huh." Hannah ran her thumb over her plump bottom lip, which was enough to drive Cooper crazy. She had outrageous sex appeal in his mind — especially in the barmaid outfit, which hit every one of her curves in a manner that caused his libido to fire into overdrive — and he often found he could think of nothing but her. She didn't even have to be in close proximity for him to drift off into a daydream. His mind was often fixated on her without prodding, which was something that legitimately worried him.

"Did you hear what I said?" Hannah prodded, causing Cooper to jerk his head in her direction. Unfortunately for him, his mind had wandered again ... and right when she was in the middle of a sentence.

"I was just thinking about the new group of guests," he lied. "It's supposed to be a whole contingent, which is a lot of people. We don't generally play host to an organized group for the last tour of the day."

"I'm the one who okayed it," Hannah admitted, rueful. "The girl at the reservation office — I think her name is Sadie, although I can't quite remember — called to ask if we could arrange it because it was a local business that was running a giveaway that benefited us and I didn't see why it would be an issue. Now I kind of see why it's an issue."

He couldn't help himself from smiling. She was adorable when fighting her earnest nature, which is exactly what appeared to be on the menu this afternoon. "I wouldn't worry about it," he said after a beat. "It will all work out. The people here know what they're doing. One late night isn't going to kill us. Besides, it sounds to me as if this group is made up of return guests rather than first-time tourists. I bet that means they'll be in and out relatively quickly."

Hannah hoped that was true. She didn't want to keep her workers from their families a moment longer than necessary. "Yeah." She trailed off and flicked her attention to the window. "There's one other thing, too."

Cooper's shoulders stiffened as he girded himself for bad news. "What? Is it Astra?"

Hannah's eyes widened as his tone turned vicious. Astra Bishop was one of the evil witches who lived in the hills surrounding the town. She was one of Abigail's former students, a woman who claimed an affinity to light magic but turned dark. She was also Cooper's former girlfriend, which made for several tense conversations.

"If she's been giving you a hard time, I want to know about it," Cooper insisted.

Hannah understood where his anxiety was coming from. He was a good man caught in an untenable situation. Abigail was like a grandmother to him. She took him on when he was having issues re-assimilating to civilian life. He suffered from nightmares and anxiety at the oddest of times. He was loyal to her. His past relationship with Astra made for uncomfortable conversations, but he understood he made a mistake with the dark witch ... and it was one he continued to regret. He wouldn't make the same mistake again, which meant he would keep Hannah safe no matter what he had to sacrifice to do it.

"It's not Astra," Hannah reassured him quickly. "You don't have to worry about her. She hasn't shown her face since Leanne went off the rails and tried to kill me."

Cooper's expression darkened at the memory. The last thing he wanted was to be reminded of Leanne Cortez. As one of Astra's minions, Cooper understood the woman was dangerous long before she tried to kill Hannah. His mistake was assuming that she was acting out on Astra's orders. For once, the coven leader wasn't the one spearheading potential evil. That didn't mean he trusted Astra with Hannah's safety. In fact, far from it. Cooper assumed Astra would become more and more dangerous the longer Hannah remained in town and didn't allow her to take over as she so desperately wanted.

"What happened with Leanne was ... a tragedy," he said finally, searching for the right words. "I wish I would've realized what she was up to before you were forced to take her on like that."

Hannah stared at the strong lines of his face for a long time before shaking her head. "It wasn't your fault." She meant it. There was no way Cooper could've realized what Leanne had planned for her. "You can't blame yourself for what happened."

Even as she said the words, Hannah recognized they were a mistake. She didn't want to talk about that night any more than Cooper did. It was too late, though. She'd managed to shove her foot into her mouth ... again.

Cooper's expression was hard to read as he regarded her. "Who should I blame? I mean ... you managed to protect yourself against a dark witch who was hellbent on killing you — something I'm profoundly grateful for — but you had to kill her to do it."

Hannah swallowed hard. Even though she couldn't forget what she'd done to protect herself, it was difficult to think about. She'd taken a life. Heck, she hadn't even given it any thought before she unleashed the spell. Her instincts kicked in and it was either conjure or perish. "I know what I did."

Cooper looked pained when he noticed the expression on her face. "Oh, Hannah, I'm sorry." Instinctively, he reached across the table and grabbed her hand. "I didn't mean to bring that up again. I just ... it's not your fault." He turned plaintive. "You did what you had to do. I don't want you spending all your time dwelling on this ... which is exactly why I shouldn't have brought it up."

"It's fine." Hannah waved off the apology. "You're right about what I had to do. I don't feel guilty or anything, if that's what you're worried about."

He studied her for a long beat. That was a lie. He had no doubt about that. He hadn't known her all that long, but it was often easy to read her emotions. She wore them every second of every day. She was still struggling with what happened in the wild tempest that descended on the town that day, and he wanted nothing more than to comfort her. Unfortunately, he had no idea how to do it.

"Hannah ... ."

She shook her head to cut him off. "You don't have to make up empty platitudes to make me feel better," she reassured him. "I'm coming to grips with it. I'm ... fine. Seriously."

He didn't believe that. Now wasn't the time to pressure her, though. He had to change the subject or they would be mired in maudlin conversation for the rest of the afternoon, to the point where they were both so uncomfortable they would have no choice but to flee. That's the last thing he wanted.

"What about the cabinet?" It was the only thing he could latch onto and he almost immediately regretted going that route. Abigail left a locked cabinet in her apartment — which was now Hannah's apartment — and there were magical items inside that required Hannah's attention. She'd been frustrated with her inability to open it even though Abigail's ghost, who was still hanging around, assured her that she would be able to unlock it when the time was right.

Hannah made a face that would've caused Cooper to laugh under different circumstances. "I still can't get it open. I think I'm going to quit trying. I bet what's in there isn't even that important."

Cooper believed the exact opposite, but it was a thorny situation. "I don't see why you can't take a break," he offered, realizing with a start that his hand was still on top of hers. How did that even happen? How long had they been sitting like this? Did she think he was being a moron? "Everyone needs a break now and then."

Slowly, he drew his hand back. When he finally got up the courage to meet her eyes, he found she wasn't even looking at him and seemed distracted. Relief washed over him at the prospect. That probably meant she hadn't even realized he'd been holding her hand for an extended period of time. That was good. So, so good.

"Yeah. I'm not too worried about it." She flashed a brief smile and then got to her feet. "It looks like the final group is here." She tilted her head toward the window, where guests were starting to stream into the street. They looked excited, as if they were having a good time, and it was a good distraction. "I should head behind the bar. Will I see you before you leave for the night?"

He nodded without hesitation. Only a handful of people remained in Casper Creek after dark. He wasn't one of them. "I'll make sure to check on you before I go. Maybe ... maybe we can get dinner together or something." The invitation was out of his mouth before he thought better of it. They'd been flirting nonstop since they met. Neither one of them had taken the initiative and tried to move beyond that, though. They both seemed frightened at the prospect.

She brightened considerably. "Sure. That sounds great."

Her reaction calmed him ... at least a little bit. He'd been nervous she would shut him down. Apparently that wasn't the case. "We'll talk about it once everyone is gone." This time the smile he offered was legitimate. "I should get back to work, too."

"I'll see you in a few hours."

He winked because it seemed the thing to do. "You definitely will."

BY THE TIME THE TOUR WAS winding down, Cooper had made three passes through town. The final group wasn't the sort to cause trouble, which was known to happen when the saloon got involved. Instead, most of the late guests this evening were families ... which meant the only headache he had to deal with was a pair of squabbling brothers who both wanted to feed the horses gum. He quickly nipped that in the bud before sending them on their way, laughing as he shook his head and leaned against the paddock fence.

"Thanks for stopping them," Tyler James offered as he joined the security guru. The blond livestock coordinator seemed more amused than concerned. Of course, he wasn't the type to fly off the handle.

"I don't think the horses would've taken it, but you never

know," Cooper replied. "It does sort of look like a sugar cube."

"They eat almost anything so I wouldn't rule it out. It probably wouldn't have been harmful, but I don't like taking chances."

"I don't blame you." Cooper rolled his neck and stretched his arms above his head. The wind had picked up and there was a bit of electricity in the air. "It feels like a storm." He couldn't help being a little disappointed because he thought that might put a damper on his dinner plans with Hannah. "I didn't see anything on the radar before, but the atmosphere feels heavy now."

"It does," Tyler agreed, glancing over his shoulder when he heard a distinctive bark. Jinx, Hannah's beloved black mutt, was having a good time trying to herd the baby goats. "Be careful around them," he chided, as if the dog could understand him. "They'll bully you if you're not careful."

Cooper followed his gaze and grinned. He was fond of the dog, and not just because he belonged to Hannah and she obviously adored him. "I didn't realize you had him today."

"I offer to take him whenever Hannah has a shift in the saloon. He likes to run and it doesn't seem fair for him to be cooped up inside when I can easily watch him. Besides, he doesn't get in much trouble. His fascination with the goats notwithstanding, he's mostly happy to sun himself and watch the guests file through."

"He's a good boy," Cooper agreed, grinning as the dog wagged his tail and hopped away from one of the aggressive kids. "The goats don't seem to like him, though."

"They don't like anybody. They're little jerks, quite frankly. If they weren't such a draw at the petting zoo, I would get rid of them."

Cooper didn't believe that. Tyler talked big when it came to the animals, but he was poor on follow-through. He had a big heart and he loved the goats as much as he did the other animals. He simply liked to complain, which Cooper was used to. "Well, they're a big draw so I guess they'll have to stay."

"I guess."

They lapsed into amiable silence for a beat. They'd known each other for a long time and were tight. They were the sort of friends who didn't need words to fill in the gaps. Of course, they were also the sort of friends who liked to tease one another. That's what Tyler had on his mind when he broke the silence.

"So, when are you going to make your move on Hannah? I've never seen two people work as slowly as you guys."

Cooper scowled. "What makes you think I'm going to make a move?"

"I've seen the way you look at her. There's no doubt in my mind you're going to make a move. The longer you wait, my friend, the more combustible you two are going to become. You realize that, right?"

"Ugh." Cooper slapped his hand to his forehead. "I'm not talking about this with you."

"Because you're embarrassed that you have no game?"

"Because it's none of your business."

Tyler snorted, genuinely amused. "Oh, you're so cute. I can't wait to see how this plays out. You're both acting like flirty idiots with no courage. It's almost painful to watch."

"Oh, stuff it." Cooper's agitation was on full display. "If it's meant to be, it will happen. In fact ... ." Whatever he was going to say died on his lips when the wind started again. This time, it brought a ball of dust with it.

Tyler instantly went rigid. "That can't be good. I think you were right about the storm. I don't think it's a normal storm, though."

That was the same conclusion Cooper had come to. "No,"

he agreed, sliding through the opening of the fence. "Get the animals inside. I think most of the guests are already heading down, but I need to house the rest of them inside until this passes."

"Be careful," Tyler called out. "Make sure you find Hannah, too. She won't know how to deal with a dust storm."

Cooper's mind had wandered straight to her. "Keep Jinx with you. I don't want her worrying about him and going on a hunt."

"I've got him. You just worry about the new boss."

That's exactly who Cooper was fixated on. He had a job to do and it included keeping Hannah safe. He wouldn't fail her twice.

TWO

*H*annah was lost in her own little world in the saloon and didn't notice how dark it had gotten outside. She was getting better at serving drinks — something she never thought she would be interested in doing — and was becoming more comfortable in her environment.

Well, except for Cooper of course. He turned her insides into jelly with a smile, something she wasn't expecting. But she wasn't sure it was a good idea to get involved with anyone so soon after her most recent relationship had imploded. She'd thought Michael Dawson was a good catch when she met him in college. He came from a good family and was on the fast track to partner at his father's law firm. That's why she dropped out of college, like a complete and total ninny, and hitched herself to his wagon train.

It turned out to be a mistake, and then some.

Michael was the reason she lost her job at his father's law firm, although only after negotiating a solid severance package. She was still finding herself after spending years with him, years looking the other way as he cheated. Her self-esteem was in the toilet when she arrived at Casper

Creek. She wasn't keen on trusting another man. Of course, Cooper wasn't Michael. She recognized that from the start. She had no doubt she could trust him. He wasn't the sort of man who would betray her. That made their flirtation even more nerve-wracking. If she could trust him and she ended up falling for him — a man who had his own set of issues with betrayal — what would happen if things fell apart?

She pushed the idea out of her mind almost as soon as it entered. She was getting ahead of herself. A flirtation was not a relationship. There was every chance they would date a few times and find they didn't even like each other as more than friends. That happened to people all the time.

Of course, if she was being brutally honest with herself, she didn't think that would happen to them. There was too much chemistry for it to suddenly disappear. Still, she was unbelievably nervous around Cooper ... and excited. Her heart turned to mush in his presence and her stomach was filled with butterflies. She was just as eager as she was reticent.

Quite frankly, she had no idea what to make of any of it.

It appeared now wouldn't be the time for her to dwell on it either. She knew the second the saloon doors flew open that something was wrong. The look on Cooper's face was one of relief, although it was quickly replaced with annoyance.

"What are you doing just standing there?" he barked, catching her off guard. "Get behind the bar and hunker down. Things are about to get ugly."

Hannah was confused. "I don't understand."

Cooper had already focused on something else so he didn't answer. "Rick, help me close the big doors," he ordered to Hannah's fellow bartender. "A dust storm is rolling in and it looks to be a doozy."

Hannah's eyes widened. "A dust storm? But ... how? This is Kentucky, not Arizona. How can there be a dust storm?"

"It's a fluke of the geography," Rick explained. "It doesn't happen a lot, but it's been known to occur this time of year, especially if we go a week or two without rain ... which is exactly what we've been dealing with over the past two weeks."

Hannah quickly looked out the window, fear clouding the clear blue of her eyes. "I need to get Jinx." She started toward the door, but Cooper shot out an arm to stop her. "He's out there," she snapped. "I'm not leaving him."

"He's with Tyler." Cooper was calm. He excelled during tense situations, which is one reason Abigail was thrilled to add him to the Casper Creek team when he showed up out of nowhere. "I happen to know that for a fact because I was with Tyler when the storm started brewing. Tyler is keeping him in the barn with him."

Hannah nodded and chewed on her bottom lip as she watched the two men shut the huge doors that covered the front of the saloon. "What about the guests? Where are they?"

"They're already down the chairlift. I double-checked as I was going through. There's nothing to worry about."

Harper didn't look convinced. "But ... ."

"Get down behind the counter," he repeated, softening his stance when he saw the terror in her eyes. "It's going to be okay. I'll be right here with you. You don't have anything to worry about."

Hannah wanted to argue, but she knew better. She was out of her element and he knew exactly what he was doing. There was nothing for her to do but acquiesce ... so that's what she did.

THE STORM BLEW THROUGH WITH ENOUGH ferocity

that it shook the buildings. Hannah huddled behind the bar and tried to hide her fear from the men with her. Cooper wouldn't allow her to endure the storm alone, though. Once they were finished with the doors, he joined her in the safest spot in the building. Cooper sat next to her, slid an arm around her shoulders, and tugged her close. His warmth and strength soothed her frazzled nerves, allowing her to relax for the full forty-five minutes they were trapped. By the time they had the doors open again and hit Main Street, she was relatively calm.

"We have to check for damage, right?" she asked Cooper as they exited the building.

"It should be okay," he reassured her. "All the buildings have dust shutters and we engaged them before I came to you. Don't freak out."

She rolled her eyes. "I don't freak out."

He cocked an eyebrow, genuinely amused. "Uh-huh. That's just what I was thinking. You never freak out, which is why you were shaking for the first five minutes we were behind the bar."

Hannah had news for him. Not all of the shaking was because of the storm. However, she didn't admit that to him. His ego was big enough for ten people as it was. "I'm fine." Her eyes flashed with annoyance. "I don't need to be protected."

"Of course you don't." He rested his hand on the center of her back and prodded her forward. "Let's check on Jinx first, huh?"

Hannah made a face. It was as if he was reading her mind. "I'm sure he's okay." She squared her shoulders as they turned in that direction. "I'm not some helicopter dog mommy who melts down all the time. I'm calm ... and collected ... and totally cool."

He pressed his lips together to keep from laughing at her

15

reaction. She was, without a doubt, one of the most amusing people he'd ever crossed paths with. She was beautiful, sweet, and said outrageous things. He absolutely adored her ... which made his heart roll with realization. If he was already this attached to her, how much worse would it get? He didn't want to think about that. "I'm sure he'll be happy to see you."

Tyler and Jinx were in the paddock when they arrived and the dog let loose an excited yip when he saw his mistress. He abandoned Tyler without a second thought and barreled toward Hannah's diminutive form. Tyler looked alarmed until he realized they were no longer alone, his lips curving up when he watched the large dog practically take the legs out from under Hannah as they collided.

"Who is a good boy?" Hannah cooed as she hugged the dog's scruffy neck. "Were you afraid of the storm? I bet you weren't. You were brave, weren't you?"

"He hid with the goats," Tyler volunteered, smirking when Cooper chuckled. "Actually, he hid behind the goats. I don't think he's all that brave when it comes to the elements."

"He's always brave," Hannah countered, momentarily burying her face in the dog's fur and taking solace in his sloppy kisses. He was fine, so she was fine. He was the one thing she took from her previous relationship that had any value. The dog was her best friend and she loved him like a child.

"He looks fine," Cooper noted, fondling the dog's ears. "I told you that worrying was unnecessary."

"Yes, you know absolutely everything," Hannah muttered. "I freak out and you're cool as a cucumber."

"I don't particularly consider cucumbers cool."

"You know what I mean."

He squeezed her shoulder. "I do. He's fine. You're fine. Everything is fine. I told you it would be and I came through on my promise. You have nothing to worry about."

Hannah didn't immediately respond, which allowed Cooper and Tyler to exchange amused looks. Tyler opened his mouth to say something — Cooper was convinced it would be something obnoxious — but he didn't get the chance. The sound of someone yelling caught the attention of both men.

"That's Aiden," Tyler noted, sobering as he watched the young man dressed as a bank robber race in their direction. "This doesn't look good."

With a sinking heart, Cooper silently agreed. He stepped in Aiden's direction and held up his hands to calm the young man when he finally arrived. "Take a breath. What's wrong?"

"It's ... bad." Aiden gasped and bent over at the waist, resting his hands on his knees so he could suck in oxygen. "It's really bad."

Cooper straightened and stared down the street. He didn't have the best view of every structure, but nothing looked out of place. "What happened? Did something collapse? Has one of the roofs collapsed?"

Aiden shook his head, still sucking in air.

"What is it?" Cooper internally cringed at how sharp the question came out and immediately adjusted. "Just tell me what's going on."

"We thought everything was fine," Aiden started. "Everyone disappeared inside like we usually do during a dust storm. We didn't see anything until we came outside of the bank."

"What did you see?" Tyler queried. "Did something happen during the storm?"

Aiden bobbed his head. "Yeah, something terrible happened. There's a body."

Cooper's shoulder jerked. "A body? One of our people? Who is it?"

"It's not one of our people. It's a guest."

"But ... how? They were all gone."

"I don't know how, but it's definitely a guest ... and he's definitely dead. You have to come right now."

Cooper nodded without hesitation. "Take me to him. Maybe it's not as bad as you think."

Aiden wasn't about to be placated. "Oh, it's definitely bad. You're going to have to see that for yourself, though."

IT WAS MOST DEFINITELY BAD. The man on the ground, his eyes staring toward the sky although they could no longer see anything, wasn't a member of the Casper Creek acting troupe. He was dressed like a tourist and somehow had managed to escape Cooper's earlier search.

Protocol insisted that Cooper call the local authorities. James Boone, the county sheriff, arrived within twenty minutes and immediately headed for Cooper. When he saw the body on the ground, he was grim.

"How did this happen?"

Cooper shrugged and held out both hands palms-up. "I have no idea. We took cover during the storm. He was here when it passed."

Boone was all business. "Did you search the town for guests before taking cover?"

Cooper bristled. "No, I decided to hide under an umbrella and save myself."

Boone shot him a chiding sidelong look. "I wasn't being negative. I'm simply trying to figure out what happened here. You know how this works."

Cooper heaved out a sigh and let his shoulders sink. "I'm sorry. I wasn't trying to be difficult. It's just ... I checked. I don't understand what he was doing up here."

"I think I can answer at least part of the question," a voice announced from the nearby blacksmith storefront. There,

Arnie Morton slipped through the door and allowed his gaze to bounce from face to face. "Is everybody okay?" His gaze lingered on Hannah, who had been largely silent since the discovery of the body.

"Everyone is fine," Cooper reassured him. "Except this guy, who we need answers on. You said you had answers."

"Not all of them," Arnie countered. "I just got a call from the bottom of the mountain, though. Ben is running the chairlift today. They took cover down there, too, even though it was nowhere near as bad as here. Communications were down for a bit because the dust wreaks havoc with cell signals, as you well know."

Cooper feigned patience as he waited. Boone was another story.

"You tell stories like my daughter," Boone complained "Just get to it."

Arnie, who had his role as crotchety old man down pat, shot a quelling look in the sheriff's direction. "I'm getting to it. There's no need to be a pain."

Boone rolled his eyes. "Just tell us what you know."

Arnie nodded, his eyes traveling back to Hannah before ultimately landing on Cooper. "Ben had been calling for a full forty-five minutes but couldn't get through. He wanted us to know that one of the guests didn't make it to the bottom of the mountain.

"A woman is down there, Lindsey Lincoln," he continued. "She was with her husband and two sons on the mountain. She went down in a lift with them and the husband, Todd, was supposed to follow. He never did."

Cooper's eyes moved back to the body. "I'm guessing this is Todd."

Arnie shrugged. "I have no idea. They're heading back up to look for him, though. I thought you would want to know."

Cooper was grim. "Oh, well, that's just great. That sounds exactly like what I want to deal with right now."

LINDSEY WAS A SOBBING MESS WHEN Boone intercepted her and directed her toward the saloon. He took the time to check the victim's wallet to confirm his identity and then broke the bad news to the wife. She didn't handle it well.

"How is this possible?" Tears streaked her cheeks as she made a series of guttural sounds that ripped Hannah's heart to shreds. She had no idea what to do regarding the situation, but she felt woefully out of her depth.

"We're not sure yet," Boone replied. "We'll be doing a full investigation. The medical examiner is on the way and he'll have to conduct an autopsy because there are no obvious signs of damage to the body."

"What does that even mean?"

From behind Lindsey, two boys — they'd been introduced as Patrick and Logan and looked to be about twelve and ten respectively — remained silent. It was obvious they were bewildered and they had no idea what to do given their mother's understandable breakdown.

"I don't have any information for you," Boone replied. "We're still confused how your husband managed to go undetected. The town was searched before everyone shut down for the storm."

Lindsey was incredulous. "Are you blaming him?"

Hannah stirred, finally finding her voice. "Of course not. We would never blame him. We're simply trying to sort out the facts."

Slowly, deliberately, Lindsey tracked her eyes to Hannah. There was accusation there ... and unimaginable grief. "And who are you?"

"This is Hannah Hickok," Boone volunteered quickly. "She's the owner of Casper Creek ... at least for the past few weeks. Her grandmother used to own the venue and passed it on to her when she died."

"I see." Lindsey's tone was clipped. "I'm assuming this is the woman I will be suing for my husband's death. That's good to know."

Hannah's heart gave a little jolt. She hadn't even considered that. "I'm so sorry." She was at a loss for words. "I know this has to be a trying time for you."

"A trying time?" Lindsey was practically screeching. "My husband is dead. Two hours ago he was fine. He was supposed to be right behind us on the chairlift. Now he's dead and I'm a single parent. I would definitely say that's trying for me."

Hannah worked her jaw, at a loss.

"Mrs. Lincoln, we can't fathom what you're going through," Cooper reassured her quickly, smoothly sliding in front of Hannah to take the bulk of the grieving woman's wrath onto his broad shoulders. "There's little we can say to give you comfort. We would never pretend otherwise.

"I don't know what to say to you other than we will find out what happened," he continued. "That won't make your family whole, but we won't stop until we have the answers you need. Ms. Hickok is not at fault, though. She didn't kill your husband."

"And what did?" Lindsey got to shaky feet and clutched her purse. "Are you saying a dust storm killed him? I have my doubts about that. I think it was your negligence that killed him."

Cooper looked as if he was going to say something else, but Boone shot him a small, almost imperceptible headshake and Cooper took the hint.

"Mrs. Lincoln, I will be in charge of this investigation,"

Boone reassured her. "I will most definitely find out what happened to your husband. Have no doubt about that."

"That won't make things better." She moved toward her children, who hadn't said a single word since being herded into the saloon. They looked shell-shocked. "You'll be hearing from my lawyer, Ms. Hickok. I can guarantee that."

Hannah didn't say a word. There was really nothing she could say. Instead, she merely stood against the wall, her hands clasped in front of her, and watched as the woman herded her children out of the building.

Her heart went out to the young boys. They'd left their house this morning, assuming they were going on an adventure, and they'd lost their father along the way. They were bound to be traumatized.

As if feeling her eyes on him, the younger boy — his mother introduced him as Logan, she reminded herself — turned in her direction. She expected to find grief in his somber eyes. Instead she found glee. They glowed red for an instant, as if sending a warning, and then the boy was back to looking like a normal child.

He didn't glance in her direction again as his mother dragged him from the building. Then he was gone, and all Hannah could do was wonder if she really saw what she thought she saw.

THREE

She was the only one who noticed. A quick glance at Cooper and Boone told her they were oblivious to what had happened ... which made her wonder if she was losing her mind.

"We can't do anything until we have the autopsy results," Boone explained. "For all we know, he had a heart attack. It could very well be natural causes. There were no marks on the body."

"Is that what you're leaning toward?" Hannah asked finally, her voice raspy.

Cooper quickly shifted his eyes to her. She sounded worn down, as if she were about to fall asleep on her feet. She looked ragged to boot and all he wanted to do was sweep her up in his arms and coddle her. "You shouldn't be worried about this," he said automatically. "Odds are that there was nothing we could've done to prevent his death."

Hannah was understandably dubious. "Really? Do you have a lot of natural deaths up here? I must've missed that particular highlight advertised in the brochure."

Cooper reminded himself that she was partially in shock

given everything that had happened and refrained from snapping at her. "I don't know that I would say we've had a lot of natural deaths. It's not unheard of, though. We've had a few heart attacks ... one guy went down with an aneurysm that most certainly wasn't our fault. That could've happened in this instance, too."

Hannah understood that he was trying to make her feel better, but she didn't want to know about the best-case scenario. It was the worst-case giving her fits. "What happens if we're at fault?"

Boone and Cooper exchanged weighted looks but neither answered.

"What happens?" Hannah repeated, more forceful this time.

"You most likely wouldn't be facing charges if it was an accident," Boone replied finally. "Accidents happen, after all. Your insurance company might pull coverage, though. That was always a concern for Abigail. She was terrified she would lose coverage because you can't operate if you don't have an insurance provider willing to take you on."

Hannah nodded, her mind busy. "When will you know what he died of?"

"Hopefully tomorrow."

"Then I guess there's nothing we can do until tomorrow." She dragged a hand through her hair, which had come loose from her earlier bun. She'd thought it looked perky when she caught a glimpse of her reflection. Now, when she looked at her reflection in the mirror behind the bar, she saw nothing perky about her countenance. "What should we be doing to clean up the town?"

"Nothing," Cooper replied, concern washing over him. She already sounded defeated, which was something he didn't want to see. "It's supposed to rain tomorrow morning.

The workers will arrive early to clean up. There's nothing you have to do."

"Well ... then I guess I'll head out to take a look around and collect Jinx." She shuffled toward the swinging doors. "Just let me know what needs to be done, Sheriff. I'll take care of it."

Boone nodded as he watched her go, thoughtful. "It's going to be okay, Hannah," he said finally. "We'll figure it out."

"You're not alone," Cooper added. "We're all in this together."

Hannah appreciated the words, but they sounded empty. She'd never felt so alone in her entire life.

Boone waited until she disappeared into the growing gloom outside to speak. "She seems shaken."

"Do you blame her?" Cooper's tone was accusatory. "She's never had to deal with stuff like this before. She's doing the best she can."

Boone's gaze turned speculative. "Did you get the feeling that I was attacking her?"

"I ... don't know." Cooper turned sheepish. "She's just dealing with a lot."

"And you see her as a wounded bird you need to tend," Boone surmised. "I get it. Believe me, I get it. She's not weak, though. Forget the fact that Abigail was her grandmother — and that woman was stronger than any ten men put together — but we've seen her in action. She's strong. You can't coddle her, no matter what your instincts tell you to do."

Cooper scowled. "I'm not coddling her. Why do you think I'm coddling her?"

"Because I'm a man and I recognize the instinct. I often want to coddle my daughter, too, but that's rarely the smart move. I want my daughter to be strong — like Hannah is strong — so I can't always make things better for her. I have to trust that she'll do it for herself. You need to do the same for Hannah."

"And what makes you think I'm not?"

"I didn't say you were doing anything wrong. I'm just suggesting that you let her absorb this herself for a bit. I think she'll be better off for it."

Cooper was dour. That wasn't what he wanted to hear. "I'll consider it."

"That's all I ask."

ONCE HANNAH RECLAIMED JINX FROM ARNIE, who was feeding the dog biscuits from a box and having a regular conversation with the animal, as if Jinx would somehow magically start answering, she didn't point herself back toward the saloon. Although part of her wanted to go to bed, hide under the covers, and hopefully wake up in a world where this had all been a dream, she knew better than falling apart. She had to hold it together ... and figure this out.

With that in mind, she sought out Jackie Metcalf, the woman who served as a seamstress for Casper Creek's ornate costumes. She was a lovely woman, friendly, and always served as a calm sounding board when Hannah needed someone to talk to. She was also a witch, and what Hannah needed more than anything was to figure out if she'd actually seen something evil within Logan Lincoln.

"I heard about the body," Jackie announced as she swept the front porch of the haberdashery store. "That's crazy, huh? Does Boone have any idea what happened to him?"

Hannah shook her head. "No. He says they won't know until the autopsy is complete tomorrow."

"That's a bummer."

Hannah could think of a few other words for it. "Yeah, well ... um ... I have a question for you."

Jackie shifted so she could study Hannah's wan features and wanted to kick herself for not realizing the woman was obviously struggling with something. "Are you blaming yourself for this? If so, you shouldn't. He probably just had a heart attack or something. It's happened before."

Hannah arched an eyebrow, amused despite herself. "Is that the Casper Creek motto? Come for the beer, stay for the heart attack. You're the second person to tell me this has happened before. It's a little freaky."

"I don't know why it would be freaky. It honestly has happened before. People can have heart attacks anywhere. Casper Creek isn't immune."

"I get that." Hannah pressed the heel of her hand to her forehead. She could feel a potential headache brewing and it was the last thing she needed. "The thing is ... um ... ."

Jackie feigned patience for as long as she could ... and then succumbed to her baser urges. "You should just spit it out. You'll feel better when you get whatever this is off your chest. Wait ... does this have anything to do with Cooper? If so, maybe I should sit down. It's not that I don't love gossip — especially when it's of the romantic variety — but sometimes I find it tedious. I hope that's not the case this time."

Hannah rolled her eyes. "This has nothing to do with Cooper. It has to do with ... magic." The final word was difficult for her to get out. She was still growing accustomed to her new reality.

"Really?" That wasn't the response Jackie was expecting. "Okay. I'm here to answer questions about that, too. I thought it would be a bit before you came to me for answers on anything big, though."

"I thought so, too," Hannah admitted ruefully. "Something happened tonight, however, and I have questions."

"Something happened with the dead man? I hadn't heard

that anything supernatural went down during the storm. This is getting more and more intriguing."

"I don't know that anything supernatural happened," Hannah hedged. "I didn't see anything during the storm. I saw something after the storm." Going for broke, she launched into her tale. When she was done describing Logan's glowing red eyes and chilly demeanor, Jackie looked more flummoxed than alarmed.

"Are you sure that's what you saw?" she asked finally.

Hannah nodded. "I'm almost positive. Why would I imagine something like that?"

"You were in shock."

"I was surprised. I wasn't in shock. Why does everyone here insist on treating me like a mental invalid? I can handle things. I think I've shown that on more than one occasion."

Jackie's lips curved. "I wasn't suggesting that you're weak. You're new to the magic game, though. You were also under duress because the widow threatened a lawsuit. You're worldly and understand about things like that. It still had to come as a shock."

"Oh, *that*." Hannah pressed her lips together and considered the statement. Finally, she nodded. "I guess I was a little shocked. It wasn't enough that I would imagine those eyes, though. There has to be another explanation."

"Well ... there's only one that I can think of."

"Really?" Hannah perked up exponentially. "What reason?"

"He's a demon."

That wasn't the answer she was expecting. Not by a long shot. "What?"

Jackie chuckled at Hannah's reaction. "Sit down. I have a few things to explain to you. I'm not sure what you really saw, but if we are dealing with a demon, there're a few things you should know."

Hannah dumbly nodded. "Okay." She felt weak in the knees as she sat on the barrel across from Jackie. "Are demons honestly real?"

She nodded. "Yeah, and they're not the easiest of foes to take on. If we have a demon problem, it's going to take all of us working together to deal with it."

"Could it be something else?"

"Not that I've ever heard of. It's probably a demon ... which means we have even bigger things to worry about than a dead body."

To Hannah, that was a sobering thought. "Okay, lay it on me."

"Just remember ... you asked for it."

THE DEMON CONVERSATION DIDN'T go exactly how she thought. By the time she returned to the saloon it was empty except for Cooper, who had a bag of food and was sitting at one of the tables. His expression was hard to read.

"I thought you forgot about me."

Caught in a reverie, it took Hannah a moment to shake herself out of it. "Oh, I ... what's that?"

"Dinner. I thought we agreed to eat together."

She'd forgotten, which horrified her. "I'm so sorry. I got caught up talking to Jackie. I didn't mean to ... ." She didn't finish the sentence because she was afraid of coming across as rude.

Cooper wasn't going to let her off that easily. "You didn't mean to forget me?"

"I just got caught up. I'm so sorry. I would never forget you. Things just took me by surprise tonight. I ... am so sorry."

Because he couldn't take torturing her a second longer, Cooper let out a long sigh and shook his head. Then he smiled. "I was just messing with you." His grin was impish. "I knew you were with Jackie. I saw you. The conversation looked intense so I didn't want to interrupt."

Hannah's lips curved down. "You are not even remotely funny."

"Sure I am. I also arranged to get burgers and fries for both of us."

Hannah cocked a dubious eyebrow. "How did you manage that?"

"I paid Aiden ten bucks to pick it up for us. He says he needs video game money."

"You're so smart." She moved closer to the table, wondering how she was going to explain that she'd lost her appetite. When she got a whiff of the food, however, she practically started drooling and forgot about anything else. "That smells heavenly."

"I'm glad." He motioned toward the chair across from him. "Why don't we eat down here? It's a nice night despite the earlier storm and the rain is due to come in overnight so we might as well enjoy the fresh air while we can."

"That sounds like a plan."

The next few minutes were conducted in silence and Hannah had a mouth full of burger before she spoke again. "You didn't have to do this. It's going above and beyond."

The fact that she was so hungry she was talking with her mouth full amused him. "It's fine. I was hungry, too. It's better eating with you than eating alone."

She swallowed. "You still didn't have to go out of your way for me."

"I didn't go out of my way for you. I did what I wanted to do."

"That's kind of sweet."

He winked. "That's what they all say." He dunked a fry in

ketchup and eyed her speculatively "What were you and Jackie talking about?"

"Oh, well ... ." She felt uncomfortable under his keen gaze and focused on her food.

"You don't have to tell me if you don't feel like it. I was simply curious. Maybe it's none of my business."

"It's not that," she offered hurriedly. "It's just ... I'm afraid you're going to laugh at me."

"Try me."

"Well ... you know those little boys that were in here?" She barreled forward when he nodded. "The younger one had glowing red eyes."

Cooper had a mouth full of hamburger when she blurted it out and he almost choked. After falling into a coughing fit that lasted a full thirty seconds, he drank from his bottle of water, and his face was still red from exertion when he finally found his voice. "Excuse me?"

His tone was enough to have Hannah bristling. "Never mind," she muttered, glaring at her takeout container.

"No, don't be that way," he admonished. "I didn't mean to offend you. It's just ... I don't think I understand."

"I didn't either. I thought maybe I was imagining it."

"That's possible. You were in shock."

"Why does everybody keep saying that?" Hannah practically exploded. "I was surprised. I wasn't in shock."

"I didn't mean anything by it," he offered. "I just ... anybody would've been in shock given what happened."

"Well, I wasn't in shock. I saw what I saw. I've given it a lot of thought and I'm sure of it."

"You're sure you saw his eyes glow red?" Cooper had no idea what to say, but he was fairly certain that laughing would be a surefire way to get him kicked out of the saloon ... and maybe even Hannah's life. He had to find another route.

"I guess I'm having trouble imagining it. Can you tell me — from beginning to end — what you saw?"

Hannah was suspicious, convinced Cooper was one bad explanation away from laughing at her, but she gave it a shot. She took her time, laid everything out, and when she was finished he seemed far too relaxed to have fallen for the story.

"You don't have to tell me your opinion on things," she groused. "You don't believe me."

"I didn't say that." His eyes flashed. "It's just ... I've never heard of anything like that happening before."

"Well, maybe you don't know everything. Have you ever considered that?"

"Every day. However, I've been around the paranormal a lot longer than you. I've definitely seen more. While I would never pretend to have seen everything, I've never heard of anything remotely like this."

"Well, you learn something new every day, right? Isn't that the saying?"

"Yes, but ... what did Jackie say?" Cooper felt out of his element. While he didn't want to alienate Hannah, he also didn't want to indulge her imagination. It was entirely possible, at least from where he was standing, that she imagined it because she was overwrought. However, he knew better than voicing that opinion in front of her.

"Jackie wanted me to describe what I saw. She said it sounded like a demon and gave me the lowdown on them. I'm not sure what to believe ... but I definitely saw what I saw."

Cooper worked his jaw. "She said it sounded like a demon? Like a real-life demon?"

Hannah narrowed her eyes to dangerous slits. "She did. I'm guessing that makes it even harder for you to believe me."

"I didn't say I didn't believe you."

Hannah was taken aback. "Does that mean you do?"

He wasn't sure how to respond but his mouth opened anyway. "I don't believe in demons."

"So, you think I'm a liar."

"Don't even go there." His tone took on a growl that set her teeth on edge. "I don't think you're a liar. I just think that you've been through a lot today and you might not have seen what you thought you did."

That did it. Hannah was already on edge before sitting down. She didn't have any place to point her anger before, but she did now. "I am not imagining things!"

He held it together despite her ire. "I didn't say you were imagining things."

"That's exactly what you said."

"It is not."

"It is so."

"It is not." Cooper managed to retain control of his temper ... but just barely. "You've had a long day. It was your first dust storm. A man died and his wife is threatening to sue you. Isn't it possible you only thought you saw the kid's eyes glow red because of a trick of the light or something?"

It took everything Hannah had not to reach across the table and throttle him. "No."

"Are you sure?"

"Absolutely." She grabbed her takeout container and cradled it to her chest as she shot an accusatory look in his direction. "I think we're done here."

Now it was his turn to be angry. "Just like that? You don't like what I have to say and you're calling it quits? That's rational."

"I didn't say I was calling it quits. I simply meant we were done with dinner. I'm tired. I need some time to think."

"I think that's probably best." Now that he'd given in to his annoyance, there was no backing down for Cooper. He was angry enough that he knew he needed to take a step back. His voice was chilly. "I'll lock up down here. You don't have to worry about that."

"Great." She turned toward the stairs with a huff. "I'm not fragile and I wasn't imagining it."

"I never said either of those things."

"You thought them!"

Did he? Cooper couldn't argue with her take on things so he snapped his mouth shut. He figured it was his best shot of keeping their working relationship intact. As for the rest ... he had no idea where they stood and there was no way he was questioning her now. They both needed time, so that's what they would get.

FOUR

*C*ooper woke frustrated. He managed to shove Hannah's odd reaction to the previous day's events out of his head long enough to fall asleep, but her accusatory eyes and saucy attitude haunted him in his dreams. When morning came, he felt more exhausted than when he went to bed.

That put him in a foul mood when he went to work.

"What's your problem?" Tyler asked as he led the animals from the barn to the paddock the next morning. One of the tiny goats ignored his buddies and immediately raced to Cooper so he could butt him in the thigh with gusto.

Amused despite himself, Cooper stared down at the enthusiastic creature and shook his head. "I can see why Jinx is so irritated by these guys."

"Jinx loves those guys," Tyler countered. "They play together, wrestle, and chase each other. Jinx is good with them, especially for a dog that wasn't raised on a farm and could easily hurt the babies."

"I thought you said he was being a pain."

"He's got a lot of energy, but he's rarely a pain." Tyler

tilted his head to the side and regarded Cooper with a searching look. "What's up with you?"

Cooper was taken aback. "What makes you think anything is up with me?"

"Because you're morose, as if you're about to have a pity party for one."

"Well, you're mistaken." Cooper quickly averted his gaze and focused on the goat. "Does he have a name?"

"Sherlock. They were all named after book characters ... and you're definitely morose. What is it?"

Cooper balked. "I am not morose. Stop saying that word. I'm totally fine."

Tyler wasn't convinced. "I saw you deliver takeout to Hannah last night. I thought it was cute."

Cooper didn't say a word, instead planting his hands on his hips and staring at the horizon. The sun hadn't completely risen yet but was warm and inviting all the same. It made for a breathtaking view, which Cooper could pretend to focus on rather than his friend.

"You left fairly quickly," Tyler noted. "I figured you would hang out with her for an hour or two. That didn't happen. Once you left, I could see her through the curtains upstairs. She seemed to be pacing ... and she was up for a decent amount of time."

Cooper's gaze was sharp as he studied his friend. "You spied on her?"

Tyler chuckled, genuinely amused. "No. There are only a few of us who stay up here after dark. I was worried about her and I could see her window from down here. I wanted to make sure she was okay after the body incident. That's a lot for her to deal with in a short amount of time, especially after Leanne."

Cooper's stomach did a slow roll. "She doesn't really talk about it."

"Leanne?"

He nodded, blowing out a sigh. "I've tried to get her to talk about it a few times, but she's not into it. I don't want to push her. I figure she'll open up when she's ready."

"Magic as a whole is new to her." Tyler turned pragmatic. "She didn't know magic was a real thing until she moved here. Not only did she find out it was, but she also found out she had some at her fingertips to utilize. It's one thing to put on a light show. It's quite another to take a life."

Cooper shifted from one foot to the other, uncomfortable. "She had to do it. She would've died otherwise."

"I know that. You know that. It must be hard for her to swallow that."

"Yeah." Cooper dragged a hand through his hair and briefly pressed his eyes shut. "That's not what we're fighting about, though."

Instead of being sympathetic, Tyler let loose a war whoop and pumped his fist in the air, catching his friend off guard. "I knew you guys were fighting. I could tell. How can you be having trouble in paradise so early? You haven't even started dating yet."

Cooper's gaze turned withering. "I'm not talking to you about this."

"You most certainly are. Otherwise you wouldn't have come down here. I don't usually see you until after your third cup of coffee. I'm not an idiot. I can tell when you're worked up."

Rather than answer, Cooper made a grumbling sound deep in his throat.

"You know you're going to tell me what's going on," Tyler prodded, not missing a beat. "I'm your best friend and you're smitten."

"I'm not smitten," Cooper protested, flustered. "That's a

stupid word, by the way. I don't know who thought of it, but I'm definitely not smitten."

"You're a smitten kitten."

Cooper extended a warning finger. "Take that back."

Amused more than worried, Tyler shook his head. "No. It's the truth and I stand by it. Tell me what's going on with Hannah. I'll try to help you."

"What makes you think anything is going on with Hannah?"

"Because I have eyes. You're both upset. If you tell me what happened, I might be able to fix it. Then you'll both feel better."

"I doubt it."

"Try me."

Cooper stared at him for a long beat and then groaned as he scuffed his shoe against the hard earth of the paddock. "You're going to think she's crazy."

Tyler arched an eyebrow. "Now I definitely want to know."

"You don't. Once I tell you, you're not going to be able to look at her without laughing."

"I'm always looking for a reason to laugh."

Another sigh slipped from between Cooper's lips and he made up his mind on the spot. He did need someone to talk to. In truth, that's why he visited Tyler so early. This was something he couldn't figure out on his own. "Hannah thinks she saw a demon last night."

Whatever he was expecting, that wasn't it. Tyler's eyebrows flew up his forehead. "Excuse me?"

"Exactly." Resigned, Cooper told his friend the whole story. When he was done, instead of breaking into hearty guffaws, Tyler was thoughtful. "Wait ... you don't believe that story, do you?"

Tyler held his hands out and shrugged. "I don't know

what to believe. I mean ... Hannah doesn't strike me as the hysterical sort. If she says she saw something, I have to believe that's true."

That wasn't what Cooper wanted to hear. "But ... demons aren't real."

"Jackie says they are. She told Hannah about them, right? That's what you just said. If Jackie believes in demons, it's obvious Hannah didn't make up that notion in a vacuum. Maybe it's possible.

"The thing is, it sounds to me as if Hannah doesn't know what she believes and is trying to figure things out," he continued. "You shut her down like she was an idiot even though she's still trying to muddle through the mess. It can't be easy on her because this is all new, at least from her perspective. Now, in addition to freaking out because she thinks she saw a demon, she's also grappling with you calling her a nut."

Cooper immediately started shaking his head. "I didn't call her a nut. I don't think she's a liar or anything. I told her that. It's just ... demons are so fantastical. Isn't it possible she imagined it?"

"Is that what you would want to hear when confiding in someone? She trusts you. She's bonded with you. It's clear you two are eventually going to ... stir up some magic of your own." Tyler's smile was impish. "That's not going to happen if you keep acting like this. She needs support, not derision."

Cooper opened his mouth to argue with the assumption and then snapped it shut. In truth, the animal handler had a point. He had shut her down without giving her a chance to explore her feelings. That's why he hadn't slept. His conscience was nagging him. He didn't need Tyler to tell him he made a mistake. He already knew it.

"Geez." He slapped his hand to his forehead and made a

groaning sound. "I didn't mean to screw this up. I just ... demons. I can't get past the fact that she believes in demons."

"She saw something," Tyler corrected. "Whatever it was, it was enough to freak her out. She didn't come up with the demon story. She told Jackie what she saw and was told it was probably demons. You can't blame all of this on her."

"Should I blame Jackie?"

Tyler snickered and shook his head. "You're already blaming yourself. It's written all over your face. Why don't you just head over there and make up with Hannah, huh? You'll feel better once it's done."

Cooper had already convinced himself of the exact same thing. "I'm afraid she's going to yell at me," he admitted piteously.

"If she does, you can take it. In this particular case, you have it coming."

That's exactly what Cooper was afraid of.

BOONE AND COOPER WERE IN THE SALOON, takeout containers filled with fresh breakfast open in front of them, when Hannah and Jinx made their way down the stairs. The dog, who was ready and raring to go, bounded toward Cooper and made a big show of showering him with kisses as he pranced next to the table.

"Jinx, leave Mr. Wyatt alone," Hannah intoned darkly. "He doesn't have time for you."

Annoyance flared as Cooper ran his tongue over his teeth. "I have time for the dog," he said finally, making a big show of rubbing his hands over Jinx's large neck. "See, Jinx and I get along fine."

"I guess it's just me then, huh?" Hannah dejectedly threw herself in one of the open chairs as Boone raised a speculative eyebrow.

When neither one of them spoke again, Boone slowly nudged a takeout container in her direction. "Cooper made sure I picked up food for you on my way in," he explained. "You need to eat and keep up your strength."

Hannah's glare was dark. "Maybe I don't want to eat. Did you ever consider that?"

"Oh, geez." The annoyed sheriff rolled his eyes. "Do I even want to know what you two are fighting about? Wait, don't answer that. I'm fairly certain I don't want to hear it because it will remind me of all the romantic travails my daughter tells me about. Did I mention my daughter is a teenager, by the way? That essentially means you guys are acting like teenagers."

Hannah furrowed her brow. "I'm not the one acting like a jerk."

"No, you're acting like a big pouter," Boone shot back. He tapped the takeout container again for emphasis. "You need to eat. We have a few things to discuss."

Quickly, the anger Hannah had been hoarding like gold dissipated and all the color drained from her face. "What happened to Mr. Lincoln? Are we liable for his death?"

Boone realized too late that he'd made a mistake. "The autopsy won't be completed until this afternoon," he reassured her. "I don't know how he died. I'm going to guess natural causes, though. There's no way Mrs. Lincoln can hold you responsible for this."

"That doesn't mean she won't sue," Cooper countered, biting into a slice of bacon as he thoughtfully watched Hannah open her takeout container. He didn't miss the way her expression changed, lightened, and he was glad he thought ahead to have Boone bring blueberry pancakes for her.

"These smell great," she enthused, her eyes sparkling. She was actually smiling when she met Cooper's gaze, as if all was forgotten ... and forgiven. "I didn't realize how hungry I was. It's too bad there aren't more options up here for food."

"You could always cook for yourself," Boone noted, causing Hannah to make a face. "Or you could just figure out a way to get better takeout options or something."

Cooper chuckled as he wiped the corners of his mouth with his napkin. Then he turned serious. "You said you had news and you didn't want to tell me before Hannah arrived. She's here now and I want to make sure we stay ahead of this."

"Right." Boone sobered. "We talked to the people who work with Mr. Lincoln. A group of them came together because they won the trip through a competition at work."

"What kind of work did he do?" Hannah asked, her voice small.

"He was a corporate accountant for KLG. It's one of those payroll companies, where you pay them to come in and handle all the checks and employee benefits to free up your time. It's a big operation in this area and ten family trips were awarded. Lincoln won one of them. Nine other families were with him."

"Did the families stick together while they were up here?" Cooper queried. He was trying to get a picture for what happened. To do that, he had to dig into the afternoon activities.

"Mostly." Boone bobbed his head. "There were a few times some of the kids got over-excited and took off, but they were largely together."

"Did they give you any important information?" Hannah asked as she carefully spread one of the butter packets on her pancakes. She seemed unsure of herself and yet fully engaged in the conversation. Cooper took it as a good sign.

"There were a few things they said that bear investigation," he hedged. "The first is ... two of them mentioned —

independent of each other, mind you — that they thought someone had brushed up against them at some point. Then they turned and realized that was impossible because there was no one around."

Hannah had no idea what to make of the statement. "I don't understand. Is that a ghost?"

"It could be," Boone confirmed. "It wouldn't be the first time a ghost was sighted up here."

"But ... can a ghost kill a man? And, if it does, it's not as if I can use a ghost as a defense in court."

"I don't want you to worry about that." Boone swatted away her concern with a haphazard wave of his hand. "Odds are that we're going to get back a natural death ruling from the medical examiner. You shouldn't freak out, especially not yet."

Hannah understood he was trying to placate her, but she was at the end of her rope. "I don't freak out. I wish you guys would stop saying things like that. I like to think I'm pretty calm."

"You are," Cooper offered quickly. "You're very calm and level-headed."

Hannah's gaze was suspicious when it landed on him. "That's not what you said last night."

"Well, I was an idiot last night." The words were out of Cooper's mouth before he gave them much thought. Even in hindsight, though, he didn't regret them. She needed someone to bolster her and he wanted to be the person to do it. "I was tired last night and I should've listened to what you had to say."

Hannah was taken aback, but the relief washing over her was palpable. "It's okay. It was a stupid theory. I probably didn't see what I thought I saw."

"I happen to believe you." Cooper was firm. "We'll figure it out."

Hannah went warm all over at his smile and, for the first time in almost twelve hours, managed to relax. "Thank you."

Her expression pained Cooper. He had no idea he managed to roil her up the way he did and now he felt guilty. He was glad he blurted out the apology. If it gave her a little bit of peace, it was worth it. After a few minutes of quiet, where the only sounds consisted of Hannah eating her pancakes, Cooper risked a glance at Boone and found the sheriff eyeing him with overt curiosity. "What?"

Boone shook his head. "Nothing." He rolled his eyes before grabbing his coffee and taking a long drink. "I didn't say a word."

Cooper knew better but decided to change the subject rather than deal with Boone's rampant speculation. "You said you found out a few things from interviewing the other families. What else have you got?"

"Well, other than two people complaining that they brushed up against someone who wasn't really there, the only thing of interest I managed to ascertain was that Todd Lincoln was apparently in a bad mood because he kept yelling at his family."

Hannah paused with a heaping forkful of pancakes halfway to her mouth. "I don't understand. Are you saying he was verbally abusing them?"

Boone held out his hands and shrugged. "I can't answer that question. All the co-workers would say was that he was acting irritated and out of sorts. The boys ran off at one point, although they didn't go far, and he apparently made a jerk of himself by yelling at them. One of the guys I talked to said the boys were being a little rambunctious but nothing out of the ordinary."

"In other words it was the father acting out of line and not the kids," Cooper mused. "I wonder if he was enough of a jerk to enrage one of his co-workers ... or his wife. Maybe she got fed up and hit him over the head or something and threatened to sue to cover her actions."

Boone shrugged. "I don't have an answer for you. Right now, we're waiting on the autopsy. We can't do anything until we get a ruling on cause of death."

"So ... we're just expected to go back to work like nothing happened?" Hannah asked after a beat. "I mean ... will we open today like it's a normal day?"

Cooper nodded without hesitation. "It's a normal day," he insisted. "Think of it like a circus performance. No matter what, the show must go on."

Hannah tilted her head, considering, and then nodded. "Okay. I just hope we get some answers by the end of the day."

"That would be best for everybody concerned," Boone agreed. "The sooner we can put this behind us, the better."

FIVE

*H*annah wasn't ready to let go of her demon theory. Sure, it wasn't an actual theory until Jackie explained about demons, but the more she thought about it, the more she warmed to the idea. If witches were real, why not demons?

After breakfast, she walked Jinx to the stable and asked Tyler if he would be willing to watch the playful canine. He readily agreed, said Jinx was a great draw for the guests, and didn't ask about her plans. Technically, she was supposed to work in the saloon. She tasked one of the other workers to cover for her, however, and headed out.

Actually, she snuck out. The one person she didn't want to see her leaving was Cooper. While he'd been pleasant and accommodating over breakfast, she had no doubt he was still riding the "Hannah is crazy" train. She didn't want to explain what she had planned, so it was easier to just slip out.

She had to look up the family on the internet. Thankfully, she found an address. Since she wasn't familiar with the area, she plugged the information into her car's GPS and then followed the red line on the screen until she found herself in a pleasant subdivision. Once she figured out the correct house, she parked on the adjacent corner and rolled down her window before killing the engine.

It wasn't overly hot — something she was thankful for — but she regretted not buying a bottle of water from a gas station before settling in.

Truthfully, Hannah wasn't sure what she expected to see at the house. She couldn't get Logan out of her mind, though. The boy had been quiet during his mother's meltdown. She tried to put herself into his shoes, think about the things that must've been going through his head, and feel the emotions she would've felt in his place.

She came up empty. First off, he was a boy. She had zero experience with pre-teen boys. Television and movies made her think they weren't the demonstrative sort. A girl the same age probably would've been crying and carrying on. That's how she would've reacted. Neither boy showed much emotion, though. She'd initially written it off as shock, or maybe even confusion. Now she wasn't so sure.

Movement at the front of the house caught her attention. It was Patrick, the older boy, and he looked subdued. He exited the front door and headed straight for the mailbox. Hannah slid lower in her seat to make sure he didn't catch sight of her, but he didn't as much as look in her direction. He seemed focused on his task.

The closer he got the clearer the picture Hannah was able to make out. His eyes were red and puffy, indicating he'd been crying, and his features were closed and drawn. She wanted to go to him, comfort him, and yet she knew that would be the absolute worst thing to do. If Lindsey found out, she was likely to call the police ... and Hannah couldn't blame her given the circumstances. The family had been through enough.

Patrick was halfway back to the door when Logan

appeared. He stood on the front porch, his face wan, and watched his brother shuffle back. Unlike his older sibling, Logan didn't look as if he'd been crying. His face was smooth, free of the blotchy patches Patrick boasted, and his eyes weren't puffy.

She reminded herself that no two people reacted in the same manner to death. Sometimes people shut off their emotions and closed out the world. It was possible Logan was reacting that way. He was younger after all. He might simply not understand the true ramifications of what happened.

The window was down, allowing a soft breeze to waft through the car. The neighborhood was so quiet, Hannah had no problem hearing the words being exchanged by the boys.

"What's Mom doing?" Patrick asked, his voice raspy.

"She's still in bed." Logan sounded blasé, as if largely disinterested in the conversation. "I'm going to wake her up."

"Don't do that. She needs to sleep. She was up all night."

"Why?"

"Why do you think?" Patrick's agitation was on full display. "She was on the phone with Grandma until really late."

For the first time since she'd first glimpsed the younger boy — and that included the time they'd spent in the saloon the previous afternoon when he'd first discovered his father had passed away — Logan had an emotional reaction.

"Oh, don't tell me that old lady is coming here." He looked apoplectic. "I don't want to see her. She always treats me like a baby."

Patrick's response was more measured. "I don't like her either. She always says stupid stuff. Mom needs her, though."

"Mom needs a smack in the face," Logan shot back. "She's still in bed. I need breakfast."

"Make your own breakfast."

Logan looked as if that were an alien concept. "Um ... no way. I'm not cooking for myself. I'm not supposed to use the stove. You know that."

"It's probably because you almost burned the house down the last time." Patrick stilled at the bottom of the steps that led to the large porch. "You don't have to cook something. There's cereal. Just have that."

Logan rolled his eyes. "I don't like cereal. She got rid of the good stuff."

"That's because of you." Patrick's unhappiness only grew as he glared at his younger brother. "The doctor says you get too hyper if you have too much sugar and that's why we can't have any good cereal."

"I don't get hyper."

"You do so."

Hannah couldn't stop herself from smiling. Now they sounded like normal brothers squabbling about unimportant things. Of course, the timing was off, but they had so much to deal with it was nice to see.

"I still want breakfast." Logan was adamant. "She's supposed to make sure we eat. I'll starve soon if I don't have something. I'm going to wake her up."

Patrick was up the steps in two quick strides and he grabbed his brother by the back of the shirt before he could disappear into the house. "Don't even think about it." He looked serious and Hannah was momentarily worried she would have to insert herself into the argument, if only to make sure one of the boys didn't end up with an injury.

"Don't tell me what to do." Logan's voice was practically dripping with warning as he grabbed his brother's wrist. "Don't touch me either. You're not supposed to touch me. I told you what would happen if you ever touched me."

To Hannah's utter surprise, instead of pushing things

49

further, Patrick immediately released his brother and took a deliberate step back. It was hard to see the expression on his face given the angle, but she was almost positive she saw fear reflected there. That seemed out of place given the circumstances. Patrick was bigger, he had at least two inches on the younger boy, and he outweighed him by a good thirty pounds. Logan was clearly the one in control, though.

"I just don't want you to wake her up," Patrick said finally, his voice weaker than it had been only moments before. "Dad is dead. You know what that means, don't you? He's not coming back."

"So what? He was always mean anyway."

"He wasn't always mean."

"Maybe not to you. He was mean to me, though. He was mean yesterday. He kept yelling at us."

"Because you wouldn't stop breaking the rules." Patrick's words were laced with accusation. "You always break the rules. If you had just done what he said ... ."

"What?" Logan's disdain was hard to miss. He was a cocky kid and he wasn't afraid to show it. "Are you blaming what happened on me?"

"Of course not." Patrick's answer was fast, automatic. Hannah wasn't sure she believed him, though. It was obvious the dynamic between the boys was somehow off. "It's nobody's fault. It's one of those things that just happens."

"Mom doesn't think so," Logan countered. "She's going to sue that woman at the Western town. Do you think we'll be rich if she does?"

"I don't think she's going to really sue."

"Why not?"

"Because it wasn't that woman's fault either. She wasn't even there."

"Who cares?" Logan rolled his shoulders, as if preparing for a fight. "I think she should sue her. Then we won't have to hear how she can't afford to buy us what we want. I think it's a good idea."

"Well, I wouldn't get your hopes up."

"You're like zero fun." Logan shuffled back toward the door. "I hate it when you're no fun." He cast a look over his shoulder. "I'm going to wake Mom up for breakfast now. I'm hungry."

"Don't do that. I'll make breakfast for you. Mom needs to sleep. It's going to be worse if she wakes up."

"You're going to cook for me?" Logan brightened considerably. "Okay. I want pancakes."

"I'll make them." Patrick was resigned. "Just ... don't wake her up. She's going to be sad when she gets up again."

"I won't wake her up."

Hannah remained rigidly slouched in her seat until the boys disappeared inside and then she straightened. She wasn't sure what she'd just witnessed, but it wasn't normal. That was the only thing she could ascertain with any degree of certainty.

TWO HOURS LATER, HANNAH'S BACK and legs were screaming about being cooped up in the car. There had been no further activity at the house, so she risked exiting her vehicle to stretch her legs. She walked up and down the block three times and was preparing to climb back in the car when she noticed a man watching her from a nearby house. He was young, in his late twenties, and he seemed amused by her exercise routine.

"Hello." Hannah straightened, feeling like an idiot. "Um ... how are you?"

He laughed at her reaction. "I'm good. How are you?"

"I'm ... great. I'm just looking around the neighborhood because I'm interested in purchasing a house around here." The lie rolled off her tongue with little effort.

"Really?" The man's eyes gleamed with interest as he abandoned his trimming device and circled out from behind the hedge. "You would be a great addition to the neighborhood."

Up close, he was extremely attractive. He had dark hair cropped close to his head and he was shirtless, which allowed her to get a gander at his impressive muscles. He obviously worked out ... a lot. His green eyes were keen as they looked Hannah up and down, and it was clear he liked what he saw because there was an undeniable gleam in his eyes.

"I'm Derek Gibson." He wiped his hand on his shorts before extending it in her direction.

"Hannah Hickok." She had no choice but to act like a friendly real estate enthusiast, so that's exactly what she did. "This is a nice area. Have you lived here long?"

"Two years. I bought the house right after I moved to the area — I'm from Ohio originally — and I'm not sorry. This is a great neighborhood, quiet. I mean ... you like a quiet neighborhood, right?" His eyes continuously roamed over her trim body. "You're not a party animal, are you? Not that there's anything wrong with that."

Hannah had to swallow the absurd urge to laugh. It was a surreal situation, but she couldn't exactly tip her hand to the real reason she was watching the Lincoln house. Derek seemed friendly enough but that didn't mean he wouldn't report her for being a crazy stalker if he felt it necessary.

"I'm not a party animal," she reassured him. "I'm the quiet sort."

"Kids?"

She shook her head, understanding what he was really asking without having to think too hard on it. "No kids. I have a dog. That's it, though."

He visibly relaxed. "That's good. That's really good." He glanced around, his smile never wavering. "What can I tell you to get you to move to the neighborhood? I think you would be a great fit."

Since she was stuck there anyway, Hannah decided to use him as a source. "Well, what's the homeowners association like?"

He barked out a gregarious laugh that took her by surprise. "There's no homeowners association here. Let me guess, you're from a big city with a lot of suburbs. This is an older community. It's not a subdivision."

"Oh." Hannah couldn't help wondering if she should've realized that herself. "That's good. There's nothing worse than an overzealous homeowners association."

"I'll have to take your word for it. This is my first house."

"You mentioned the neighborhood is quiet." She regrouped quickly. "Does that mean it's all older couples?"

"Oh, um ... not really." Derek looked legitimately pensive as he glanced around. "The Dorchesters live in that house and they're older." He pointed toward a well-kept house with gingerbread trim on the corner. "They're the sort who sit on their front porch and spy on the neighbors. They're really worried about what everyone else is doing. They're basically harmless, though."

"That's good. What about the others?"

"Well, you have the Stinsons here." He gestured at another house. "They've been married about six months and they spent all their time banging for the first three months. They were so loud there was no way to mistake what they were doing. You could hear them from every direction.

"All that banging went to good use, though, because now she's pregnant," he continued, clearly enjoying his position as neighborhood welcome chairman. "She's not due for another six months or something, but they're constantly cooing at each other and having baby furniture delivered. They're a little sugary but harmless."

Hannah nodded, her eyes automatically tracking to the Lincoln home. "And there? It looks like they have kids. They're not loud kids, are they?"

Derek's smile slipped. "They have two boys. Twelve — although I think Patrick is almost thirteen now — and ten. They're not overly loud. They play in the yard sometimes and Patrick has some friends who come over and play basketball about once a week. Logan, well, he's not loud at all."

The way he said it piqued Hannah's interest. "I've never heard of a ten-year-old boy being quiet."

"Logan is. He just kind of hangs around by himself. He doesn't have any friends."

"None?"

"Nope." Derek shook his head, a look of melancholy washing over his features. "They're honestly good boys. They don't get into a lot of trouble."

He was obviously leaving something out of the telling, Hannah surmised. She was more determined than ever to figure out what. "There's something you're not saying."

"Oh, well ... ." Derek let loose a terrific sigh. "The thing is, their father was the loud sort. He would yell quite often even though the boys weren't doing anything wrong. I think he was one of those crabby guys who was never going to be happy no matter what those boys did. I recognized it in him because my father was the same way."

Hannah pursed her lips, sympathy welling up. Her father was the exact opposite. He was the enthusiastic sort and almost never yelled. The one instance she could remember of him losing his temper happened when she was a teenager and a man tried to pick her up outside the mall. She'd been naive, didn't realize what was happening, and her father absolutely lost it when he showed up. After the fact, he reassured her he wasn't angry with her but afraid of what might've happened. After that, she'd been much more careful when it came to strange men.

"You're talking about the father in the past tense," she noted after a beat. "Did something happen?"

Derek nodded, his eyes never leaving the house. "Apparently Todd died yesterday. That's the rumor I heard anyway. He was out on some family gathering and he just dropped dead."

Hannah widened her eyes because she figured that was the appropriate response. "Do they know what happened to him?"

He shook his head. "Not that I'm aware. I'm betting it turns out to be a heart attack or something. He was the high-strung sort."

"That's horrible."

"Yeah. I feel bad for the boys ... and Lindsey. That's the mother. I think Todd was the disciplinarian in the family and she was the more indulgent parent. I think she's going to have a lot to deal with going forward. Raising two boys ... I mean, they're good boys. It's just a different world today than she was dealing with yesterday."

"I can imagine." Hannah licked her lips. "Well, you've definitely given me a lot to think about. I like the neighborhood, but I need to have a sit-down with my bank and make sure I can finance the house."

"I hope it works out." Derek's smile was back. "In fact, before you go, what do you say to me buying you lunch? There's a restaurant right around the corner that way and it's really good. If Sandy's cooking — she's the owner — doesn't convince you this is the neighborhood for you, I don't know what will."

He was eager — ridiculously so — and Hannah didn't

want to hurt his feelings. There was no way she could waste an afternoon having lunch when she was expected somewhere else, though. "Oh, well, I really appreciate it." She searched for the appropriate way to let him down easy. "I have somewhere I have to be, though."

"Where's that? It can't be that important. Come on. Take a chance." His smile was compelling and Hannah was considering acquiescing when a third shadow appeared on the sidewalk to her left, momentarily snagging her attention.

"She already has lunch plans," Cooper announced, coming out of nowhere and stealing the breath from Hannah's lungs. "I'm sure she's grateful for the rundown of the neighborhood. I'll take it from here, though."

Hannah swallowed hard. She had no doubt things were about to take a turn ... for the worse.

SIX

*D*erek's confused expression was enough to tug at Hannah's heartstrings. When juxtaposed with Cooper's stony countenance, however, she wisely bid Derek farewell — promising she would seriously consider moving to the neighborhood — and then let Cooper direct her down the street. He held it together until they reached the corner ... and then he practically exploded.

"What are you doing out here? Are you crazy? If Lindsey Lincoln sees you she can call the police."

Hannah made a face. "I just wanted to take a look. I wasn't doing anything bad."

"You're spying on a grieving widow."

"Actually, I was spying on the kids."

"That doesn't make it better."

"Yeah, well ... I just wanted to see." She rolled her neck until it cracked and glanced down the street. Derek had returned to his yard work, his clippers in hand, but his attention was clearly on them. "You didn't have to be mean to him. He was harmless."

"Please." Cooper rolled his eyes. "I know exactly what that guy was thinking. Trust me. I did you a favor."

"I could've handled myself."

"Well, I handled it for you."

She scowled at his profile. "You're not the boss of me," she announced. "In fact, I'm technically the boss of you."

"Not really."

"I sign your paychecks."

"Have you signed any paychecks yet?"

"That's neither here nor there." She didn't like his tone. "I'm an adult. I'm allowed to make decisions for myself."

"I never said otherwise. I wasn't trying to infringe on your dating prospects." He said the words with obvious disdain. "I'm trying to make sure you don't get yourself in trouble."

"I'm not going to date him. Don't be ridiculous."

"It didn't look that way to me."

"Yeah, well—" She broke off, something occurring to her. "Hold up. What are you doing out here? Why aren't you at Casper Creek?"

Cooper was taken aback by the question. "What does that matter?"

"I want to know."

"I'm just ... out for a drive."

"You're just out for a drive?" Hannah was dubious. "Why would you possibly come to this neighborhood? I mean ... the odds of you stumbling across me in this neighborhood by accident must be astronomical."

Cooper refused to meet her gaze. "Don't worry about it."

"Oh, I'm going to worry about it." She shifted from one foot to the other, her eyes going to a spot on the next block, to where his truck was parked. Then things became clearer. "You're here to watch the kids, too. You might not believe me, but you're curious enough to check things out for yourself."

"I didn't say I didn't believe you." Cooper's temper was back. "Stop insinuating that I don't believe you. I don't like that."

"Oh, well, if you don't like it." She rolled her eyes and folded her arms across her chest. "Admit you're doing the same thing I am."

"I'll do nothing of the sort."

Hannah wasn't going to let him off the hook that easily. "Admit it."

"No."

She stared at him for a long beat and then threw her hands in the air. "Fine. Be a stubborn pain. That's what you're good at. I'm leaving."

"Good. I think that's the best idea you've had all day. Wait." He reached out to grab her arm before she could storm away. "You're going back to Casper Creek, right? You're not going to pretend to leave and then circle back around, are you?"

"Of course not. If I wanted to do that, though, there's nothing you could do to stop me."

"Oh, I know." Cooper's gaze was dark when it finally snagged with hers. There was fire in her eyes, something he was thankful to see, but there was also something else. "I really am trying to look out for you."

In her heart, Hannah understood his motivations. That didn't mean she could excuse his actions. "You're not the boss of me," she reminded him. "I'm allowed to make decisions for myself."

"Fine."

"Good."

"Great."

They glared at each other for an extended beat and then turned away at the exact same time.

"I'll see you back in town," Cooper called out.

"Maybe you will."

"Don't make me have to come back here."

"Just ... mind your own business."

"As long as there's an active investigation at Casper Creek, you are my business."

"That can change."

"Oh, whatever."

HANNAH TOOK THE TIME TO stop at a fast food restaurant in town. She loaded up on a chicken sandwich, onion rings, and a malt before returning to Casper Creek. The hour of downtime was enough to have her rethinking her actions ... and she wasn't feeling good about herself when she landed in the employee parking lot.

It was obvious from the hustle and bustle around town that they were in the middle of a tour. She took a few moments to lean against a sign post in the shade and watch the gunfight that happened three times a day — the town's fake sheriff facing off with the resident bank robber — and marveled at the energy the performers expended. She'd witnessed at least thirty of these shows at this point and never once did the performances dip. If the actors grew tired, or disenfranchised with doing the same thing over and over again, they never showed it.

"Entertaining, huh?"

Hannah shifted her eyes to her right at the sound of the new voice. She was surprised to find Boone lounging on the other side of the tree, watching the show. "Are you still here? I thought you left."

"Actually, I'm back." He looked grim. "I have some news."

Hannah's heart skipped a beat, her earlier agitation with Cooper flying out the window. In this instance, she wanted nothing more than someone to lean on. Her mind immediately went to him as she sucked in a breath. "I'm not going to like this, am I?"

"No." Boone was blunt, which she generally preferred, but she would've been more comfortable with the soft sell this time. "The autopsy results came back. The cause of death is undetermined."

Hannah wasn't sure what to make of that. She'd worked in a law office for years and was familiar with criminal prosecution terms and conditions. Boone's reaction had her baffled this time, though. "I don't understand," she hedged. "What does that mean?"

"It means that the medical examiner's office needs a second opinion."

"From where?"

"The state pathologist is being called in." Boone's expression was sympathetic. "We're still okay," he reassured her. "The good news is that our guy could find no signs of foul play."

Hannah could read between the lines. "He couldn't find natural causes, though, either. That means the death will be recorded as unnatural unless the state pathologist finds something."

"Yeah," he sighed. "I'm sorry. Do you know what that means?"

Hannah nodded numbly. "If the death is recorded as undetermined, it will give Lindsey Lincoln an opening to sue me."

"Pretty much. She probably won't win but there's always a chance, with the right jury, that they'll do something stupid. I'm sorry."

"Yeah, well ... there's nothing I can do about it." She wiped her hand against her forehead. It was barely one o'clock and yet she was ready to call it a day. "When will we know the pathologist's determination?"

"I don't know. He's coming up here after the final performance of the day. I managed to hold him off until then. He wants to take a look around the property."

"What does he think he's going to find?"

"I have no idea."

"Well ... I don't see where I have a lot of say in the matter."

"You don't. I just wanted to make you aware."

"Thank you for that." She flashed him a wan smile. "You're going out of your way for me on this. I'm not oblivious. I just want you to know that I'm thankful for everything you're doing."

"You don't need to be thankful. It's part of my job description."

Hannah knew better than that, but she didn't want to push the issue. "Still, thank you."

"Don't worry about it." He reached over and squeezed her shoulder. "Abigail and I were close. I loved her like everyone else here. You're her granddaughter. That makes you family, too."

He didn't have to say it, but Hannah appreciated the sentiment. "I think I'm going to take a walk. Just to clear my head, you know. It's a nice day, but I'm not sure I should be around people."

"Don't go too far. Cooper will melt down if he finds out you're wandering around without supervision."

Hannah's scowl was back firmly in place. "Cooper can mind his own business."

Boone cocked a curious eyebrow. "Do I even want to know what you two are fighting about?"

"Probably not."

"Well ... just be careful. We don't want anything to happen to you on top of everything else."

"Don't worry about me. I'll be perfectly fine. Trust me."

FOR LACK OF ANYTHING BETTER TO do, Hannah made her way down to the creek. She'd only visited a handful of times — one of those times resulted in a head injury that almost claimed her life — and she'd avoided the area for the past two weeks. For some reason she wanted to visit today, if only for a few moments of tranquility.

The creek was quiet, the sun shining through the canopy of trees. She took off her shoes, rolled up her khaki pants, and immediately sank her feet into the cold water. She splashed around for a bit, content to walk and think, and then planted herself on the bank so she could close her eyes and work things out in her head.

It didn't go well. The more she thought about Logan, the more convinced she became that there was something off about the boy. She'd only seen the red-eyes phenomenon once, but that was more than enough to convince her something terrible was going on.

Hannah was so lost in thought she didn't realize she was no longer alone until the birds stopped singing. Slowly, she ratcheted herself up to a sitting position and frowned when she came face to face with the woman on the other side of the water. She would've recognized the long sheet of white hair anywhere.

"Astra." Her tone conveyed a great deal of dislike and weariness. "I'm really not in the mood to deal with you right now. If you could come back another time, that would be great."

Instead of acquiescing — or even picking a fight — the

dark witch merely smiled. "What's wrong? Did you break a fingernail or something?"

"Or something." Hannah closed her eyes. "I'm seriously not in the mood."

"Oh, don't cry, little witch," she teased, sinking to the ground on the other side of the slow-moving creek and resting her back against a tree. "I would've thought you were living the high life after what happened with Leanne. I mean ... that was impressive. I've never seen a new witch exert that much power in such a short amount of time. You must be proud."

That wasn't the word Hannah would've used to explain her feelings. "I don't want to talk about Leanne."

"And why is that? You ended her. You won. You should be crowing."

"I don't really see things the same way."

"How do you see them?"

Hannah wanted to strangle her. All she wanted was a few moments of quiet but she couldn't even manage that. "What do you want, Astra? We really have nothing to talk about. I mean ... we're not friends. In fact, you've made it very clear that we're enemies. I don't see that changing anytime soon, do you?"

"Not as long as you continue to act as lord and master over what's mine."

"Abigail left Casper Creek to me. It was never yours."

"No, you've got that wrong." Astra's eyes flashed with annoyance. "It was always meant to be mine. Abigail made a mistake when leaving it to you. Eventually, you're going to realize that and rectify the mistake. I can bide my time until then."

Hannah openly glared at the other woman. "I'm never going to transfer this property to you. If you believe that ... well ... you're crazy."

"I've been called worse things." She readjusted so she could sit more comfortably. "I'm not here to fight today, though. I've noticed the activity at Casper Creek. I'm curious what happened."

Part of Hannah thought it was a mistake to tell Astra what was going on. Knowledge was power, after all. However, Astra was a witch and Hannah needed information. Who better to supply it than a dark witch who understood about evil creatures?

"It's a long story," Hannah hedged.

"I have time."

Hannah needed very little prodding. She launched into the tale, leaving nothing out (except for her fight with Cooper because it seemed unnecessary to touch on that). When she was finished, Astra looked legitimately intrigued.

"Do you think it was a demon?" she asked finally.

Hannah held out her hands and shrugged. "That's what I was going to ask you."

"I've never crossed paths with a demon before."

The admission caught Hannah off guard. "Really?" Some of the hope she'd been gathering dissipated. "I thought if anyone could confirm my theory, it would be you."

"Sorry." Astra pursed her lips. "I believe in demons, don't get me wrong, but I've never heard of any landing in this area. It's not out of the realm of possibility, though."

"My problem is that I can't understand why a demon would take over a child," Hannah admitted. "I mean ... I've seen *The Exorcist*. I know it's a thing in pop culture. I guess I just thought it was a fabrication of Hollywood. I didn't think it could possibly be real."

"Actually, taking over the child makes sense to me," she countered. "Young minds are easier to suppress. Adults have a sense of self that children don't always have. If the demon needed a host body, that means something happened to the body it was formerly residing in. It could've been weak from being under attack and the child was the first being it crossed paths with."

"I didn't even consider that," Hannah mused, tilting her head to the side. "I guess it makes sense."

"It does," Astra agreed. "The most important thing is finding out what sort of demon you're dealing with."

"And how do I do that?"

"I would suggest asking Abigail."

Hannah opened her mouth to argue and then snapped it shut. That actually made sense. "Do you think she's ever dealt with a demon?"

"If she has, she never told me about it. That doesn't necessarily mean anything, though."

"I can't control when she shows up. It's one of those things where she just pops into existence and then back out again."

"Manifesting as a ghost takes a lot of energy," Astra explained. "She'll get better at it as time passes. For now, you'll just have to do your best."

"Yeah."

"I'll do some research, too," she offered. "It can't hurt to put a few people on this ... just in case."

Instead of being thankful, Hannah was instantly suspicious. "Why would you volunteer to help me?"

"Because a demon could be bad news for all of us," she replied without missing a beat. "We might not be friends — and I doubt that will ever change — but that doesn't mean we can't share a common enemy. A single demon can do a lot of damage to a great number of people. In fact ... ." She trailed off, her eyes going to a spot over Hannah's left shoulder.

When the blonde swiveled to see what had garnered the white-haired witch's attention, she wasn't surprised to find Cooper stalking in their direction. "Oh, great."

Astra's reaction to seeing him was much different than Hannah's. "Hello, lover," she purred, her eyes going heavy-lidded and demure. "I was hoping to see you today."

"That makes one of us," Hannah muttered.

Cooper ignored Astra's ludicrous reaction and focused on Hannah. "Really? Haven't you found enough trouble today? Why are you out here?"

"Because I needed some air," Hannah replied, hopping to her feet. She took the time to wipe the dirt and leaves from the seat of her pants before grabbing her shoes. "I'm allowed to get some air. I'm an adult."

"Yeah, Cooper, she's an adult," Astra teased. Now that there was another person to focus on, Astra had completely lost interest in Hannah. "She doesn't need you to act as her babysitter."

Cooper extended a warning finger in his ex-girlfriend's direction. "Don't add to this insanity," he warned, his temper on full display. "This has nothing to do with you."

"If we're dealing with a demon, it most certainly has something to do with me," Astra shot back. "We could all be in danger, not just your precious Hannah."

Cooper's eyes narrowed to dangerous slits. "Seriously?" He was incredulous as he fisted his hands at his sides. "Why would you tell her anything?"

Hannah was too tired to argue. "Because I needed information and you don't believe me. You think I'm making it up."

"Stop saying that!" Cooper was at the end of his rope. "I don't think you're making it up. I just ... I don't believe in demons. I'm sorry. I know that's not what you want to hear, but that's all I have to offer. That doesn't mean we're not dealing with something else."

Hannah blinked several times and then shook her head.

"I'm going back to the town. I'll leave you two to do ... whatever it is you're going to do."

Cooper wanted to follow her. The last thing he needed was to waste time arguing with Astra. He'd been down that road before and it never led anywhere good. Hannah's defeated demeanor told him he shouldn't push her at the present time, though. Instead, he wisely took a step back.

"I'll check on you later," he said finally. "I didn't mean to upset you."

"It's fine." Hannah felt hollow. "It's just been a long day."

"Get some water while you're up there," Cooper suggested. "I'll be right behind you."

"Whatever. Do whatever you want." With those words, she was gone, and all Cooper was left with was Astra and his annoyance.

It was a potent combination.

SEVEN

*C*ooper watched Hannah go with a mixture of annoyance and concern. He didn't know why she was acting like such a baby ... and an idiot ... and basically a tempestuous child. He had no intention of finding out either. He'd decided staying away from her was the best course of action ... for both of them.

"What's wrong, Coop?" Astra asked in a sing-song voice. "Trouble in paradise with your new girlfriend?"

Slowly, Cooper tracked his gaze to Astra. "What did she say to you?"

"Are you asking if she was talking about you?" Astra looked amused despite herself. "That's so very ... fifth grade."

Cooper folded his arms across his chest and continued to stare.

"She didn't ask anything basically," Astra replied on a sigh, shaking her head. "You used to have a sense of humor. What happened to that?"

"Perhaps it died with Abigail."

"Or perhaps you can't find it with this woman," Astra shot back. "You never had trouble laughing with me."

That was true, Cooper silently acknowledged. Astra was the one — along with Abigail and Tyler really — who helped him rediscover what it was like to laugh. There was more to the story, though.

"When I was with you, life didn't seem so serious," he admitted. "I didn't feel as if I had anything to lose so there was no reason not to laugh. Things are different now."

Astra frowned. "You cared about me. I don't know why you insist on denying it."

"I've never denied it. I did care about you. It wasn't the way you wanted, of course, but I did care ... until you betrayed Abigail and took off the way you did."

Astra didn't bother to hide her eye roll. "Why do you have to keep bringing that up? It wasn't a betrayal. It was a simple parting of ways."

Cooper remembered it differently. "It really doesn't matter. Abigail is gone. Hannah is here now. We have other things going on."

"I heard." Astra was back to being amused. "An unexplained death at Casper Creek. Who would've thought that possible?"

He recognized the sarcasm and it didn't sit well with him. "Hannah is having trouble dealing with it."

"Hannah is having trouble dealing with more than that," Astra countered. "She has too much going on for that teeny-tiny brain of hers."

Intrigue lit his face. "What did she say to you?"

"You're really curious, aren't you?"

"I'm really ... worried," he corrected. "She's had a full two days and I want to make sure she's okay. What did she say to you?"

Astra's gaze darkened as she straightened. "What makes you think I'll tell you?"

"Because it's the right thing to do."

"Since when have I cared about that?"

"Since ... you owe her." Cooper changed tactics quickly. "It was your acolyte whom you couldn't keep in line," he reminded her. "Leanne was supposed to be your underling and you couldn't control her. She tried to kill Hannah. You do realize, if that happens, you'll never get what you want."

Astra's expression turned black at the reminder. "Leanne was better at hiding her true nature than I gave her credit for. That's true. I could've taken her if it came to it. In fact, she should've been left for me."

Cooper let loose a derisive snort. "Oh, please. You were off in La-La Land when all of that went down. You thought you were playing me, but Leanne was playing you. I'm not an idiot."

"I wouldn't be so sure about that."

"You're just worked up because Leanne was clearly smarter than you."

"Yes, that must be it." Sarcasm practically dripped from Astra's tongue as she pushed herself to a standing position.

Sensing his opportunity to question her was disappearing, Cooper reminded himself that some evils were necessary. "Wait." He pasted a conciliatory look on his face when she shifted her eyes to him. "I didn't mean for this to turn so quickly."

"Oh, really?" Astra was instantly suspicious. "What did you think was going to happen?"

"It doesn't matter." Cooper was calm as he regarded her. "The thing is ... I need to know about Hannah. What did she say to you?"

"Hannah? That's why you're still here." Astra exhaled heavily as the truth hit her smack in the face. "You're all about Hannah now, aren't you?"

"I want to make sure Hannah is okay," Cooper clarified. That was true. He'd decided that pursuing romance was a terrible idea because she was too much work, too tempera-mental, but that didn't mean he wanted her to suffer. "She's been upset since yesterday, for obvious reasons. I want to know what she said to you."

Astra looked as if the last thing she wanted to do was cooperate. Still, she managed to hold it together ... if only to remain strong in front of Cooper. "She's convinced the child she saw yesterday is a demon."

"Oh, geez." Cooper smacked his hand against his forehead and shut his eyes. "I should've seen that coming. I'm going to need to talk to her again. This is getting out of control."

"You don't know that it's not demons," Astra argued pointedly.

"I do know that. Demons aren't real."

"How is it that you can believe in witches ... and ghosts ... and even shapeshifters, but you can't believe in demons?"

"Because I've seen those other things," he replied simply. "They've all turned out to be real ... and I've seen them. I've never even heard a single story about demons being real."

"Perhaps that's because you have trouble opening your ears."

"Or perhaps it's because they're not real."

Astra let out a sigh, the sound long and drawn out. "You're set in your ways. If you want to entice the new witch, you're going to have to give a little. I get the feeling that she's not the sort who will put up with being told what to do ... especially given her past."

Cooper narrowed his eyes. "What do you know about her past?"

"Enough to realize you're treading on thin ice."

"Since when do you want to help my dating life?"

"I couldn't care less about your dating life. I am interested in the demons, however. You might want to ask yourself why I believed her straight away and you think she's a liar. You're not going to be able to move forward until you figure that out."

Cooper opened his mouth to argue, but Astra was already turning away. He watched her go, a myriad of emotions jockeying for position in his brain. Finally, he turned on his heel and headed toward Casper Creek.

He had a lot of thinking to do.

BY THE END OF SHIFT, COOPER had pretty much come to the conclusion that he was an idiot. He'd been convinced he was making the right decision hours before when he decided that he and Hannah simply weren't a good mix. Since that time, he hadn't been able to get her out of his head ... and the more he thought about her, the guiltier he felt.

"What are you still doing here?" Tyler asked as he ambled over to the security guru. The town was almost completely empty and he was surprised to find his friend standing in the middle of the street staring at the saloon.

"What?" Cooper stirred, his eyes going wide when he realized he was no longer alone. He was usually much better at registering his surroundings, but he'd become lost in thought.

Instead of being concerned, Tyler chuckled. "I see that you're distracted."

"I'm not distracted." Cooper forced a smile. "I was just thinking. Boone says the state pathologist is coming back out here tomorrow ... and he wants the operation shut down so he can do a full investigation."

"Does Hannah know?"

"I saw Boone talking to her shortly before we shut down for the day. I'm pretty sure she's aware."

"Well ... it's not ideal but there are worse things in life. We'll get through it."

"Yeah." Cooper rubbed his jaw as his eyes went back to the saloon. He was trying to remain strong, stay away from her, and yet he couldn't ignore the pull he felt tugging him in her direction. "Did you talk to her at all?"

Tyler shook his head. "She's isolating herself from us. I think she believes that she's going to be in trouble for Lincoln's death and doesn't know how to deal with it. It's not surprising. From the brief conversations we've had, I think she was emotionally abused during her last relationship. She has a tendency to close down when things get bad."

Cooper jerked his head, surprised. "What do you mean?"

"I don't know if she's said anything to you, but her last boyfriend repeatedly cheated on her and made her feel as if she wasn't worth anything. He basically told her that if she'd been a better person, more interesting, he wouldn't have felt the inclination to cheat. She's still raw around the edges because of that."

Honestly, Hannah had opened up about her last boyfriend ... to the point where Cooper wanted to hunt him down and do great bodily harm to the man. He didn't understand how anyone could cheat on Hannah. It wasn't as if there was anything better out there. How could there possibly be? And still ... he hadn't really thought about what was going through Hannah's mind during all of this. He realized now that her emotional well-being should've been his biggest concern.

"I didn't really think about that," he admitted. "She mentioned the boyfriend ... how she made a lot of mistakes and regretted them. I didn't really think about that when she started talking about demons."

Tyler lifted an eyebrow. "Has something else happened on that front?"

Cooper caught him up, assuming the man would side with him. When the exact opposite happened, he was flabbergasted.

"If we're dealing with a demon, we're going to need help." Tyler was matter-of-fact. "I know a priest in town. I'll head in that direction tonight if he can squeeze me in."

Cooper worked his jaw. "Wait ... you don't believe this demon stuff, too, do you? I thought you were messing with me earlier."

Tyler nodded without hesitation. "I absolutely believe it. Why don't you?"

"Because it's ludicrous."

"Is it? Demons are former fire elementals. Witches are former earth elementals. There's a lot out there you haven't yet seen. That doesn't mean those creatures don't exist."

"Yeah, but ... ." Cooper trailed off. He felt like something of a ninny.

"There's evil and good in the world," Tyler offered. "Just like there are evil and good witches, there are evil and good demons as well. They're very real, though."

Cooper jerked up his head. "Have you seen one?"

"No, but I've heard plenty of tales. I believe in them. If Hannah thinks she saw a demon, I have to believe in her. She's never lied to us before. She's trying to figure her way around the paranormal world as much as we are. I think we owe her a little support ... especially since that's the one thing she needs to really feel like this is home."

A sick feeling settled in the pit of Cooper's stomach. He hadn't thought about that. "She's mad at me."

"Still?" Tyler looked amused rather than upset. "I guess it's good you're fairly charming and know how to fix that."

"She doesn't want to see me."

Tyler gestured toward the paddock. "She still needs her dog. I'm betting you can work that magic you have when dropping off Jinx if you're fast enough."

Cooper perked up. "Hey, now there's an idea."

"Yeah. I'm full of them."

. . .

COOPER DECIDED TO ORDER MEXICAN. He knew Hannah liked tacos — really, who didn't? — and by the time he picked up the food and collected Jinx, he was feeling better about himself.

He was also feeling nervous.

His decision to refrain from dating Hannah had gone out the window in a matter of hours. He realized now he was reacting out of anger ... and frustration. She was a difficult woman. That wasn't going to change. The best things in life required work, though, and he had a feeling she would be one of those things.

Of course, it could've had a little something to do with his hormones, too. Whenever he looked at her, his heart heaved and his stomach clenched. His body wouldn't allow him to walk away from her even if his head insisted on it.

So, he was regrouping. He had dinner and her dog ... and he was convinced he was going to make things right. One look at her face when she opened the door told him she wasn't going to make it as easy as hoped.

"What are you doing here?" Her tone was accusatory.

"I'm bringing Jinx home."

"Oh, well ... thanks." She reached out to grab Jinx's leash, but the dog had too much energy. He pushed through the partially-opened door and bounded into the apartment, endless enthusiasm on display.

"I also brought dinner," he added, holding up the bag of takeout.

"I'm not hungry." Her eyes flashed with belligerence as she jutted out her chin.

"It's tacos ... with refried beans and Spanish rice. It's that place I got our dinner a few weeks ago and you absolutely loved the food."

Hannah narrowed her eyes. "That's playing dirty."

"Yes, well ... I'll do whatever it takes to make things up to you." He opted for sincerity. Tyler said to use his charm but being honest with her seemed more important. "I'm sorry about ... well ... everything."

Hannah couldn't contain her surprise. "You're sorry?"

"That's what I said."

"I wasn't sure you knew the meaning of those words."

Instead of being offended, he chuckled. "It's come to my attention that just because I've never seen something, that doesn't mean it's not real. I got it in my head that demons couldn't be real — perhaps it was fear fueling me — and I wouldn't allow the possibility I was wrong even a minor consideration."

Hannah pursed her lips and then pushed open the door. "I guess I can accept your apology. I don't really blame you for being dubious of demons. The more I think about it, the more I wonder if I'm crazy."

"You're not crazy." He grabbed her wrist with his free hand and drew her eyes to him, earnest. "I believe you saw what you saw. I always believed that. I had trouble believing that meant we were dealing with a demon, but that hardly matters now.

"I never once doubted you saw something," he continued, searching for the right words to soothe her. "Don't think that I was questioning your sanity ... or truthfulness. You're an honest person and I know that. I'm sorry if I made you doubt yourself."

The words were better than any balm. Hannah found herself studying his features with a hunger she didn't know she possessed. Then, out of nowhere, she was on him.

Cooper caught her around the waist, somehow managing to keep hold of the food while pressing himself against her. Their lips met in an explosion of emotions —

lust being the leading factor — and all he could see was fireworks.

Most first kisses are awkward. Adjustments are often necessary. Not this kiss, though. This kiss felt like coming home ... for both of them. It went on so long, Cooper almost forgot where he was ... and what he had planned. When he finally remembered, it was with great reluctance that he pulled his head back and stared into her eyes.

His lips felt chapped they'd gone at it for so long, and his muscles felt oddly weak. "What was that?" he asked finally, finding his voice.

"I just wanted to thank you for believing in me." Hannah was breathless. "I just ... I don't know what that was."

"I kind of want to try it again," he admitted, sagging against the door frame with a loud *thud* as he kept the takeout bag in his hand and tightened his arm around her waist. "I hope that's okay with you."

Hannah let loose a giggle that was ridiculously adorable and tugged on every heartstring he had. "We can probably try it again. After dinner, I mean. I'm starving." As if on cue, her stomach growled.

Cooper raised the takeout bag. "Food first. Then we'll talk about the rest."

Hannah nodded, her eyes going heavy-lidded. "Thank you," she offered out of nowhere. "I didn't realize how much I needed you to believe in me until ... well ... you did."

He thought his heart might break at her earnest expression. "I always believed in you," he reassured her. "I never thought you didn't see something. I need you to know that. It's just ... demons. That seems somehow bigger than anything we've dealt with before."

"I definitely think there's something wrong with that boy. He doesn't react normally. I saw things this afternoon outside of the house."

Cooper nodded, thoughtful, and then pressed a kiss to her forehead. He knew if he went to her lips again they wouldn't eat and things would progress much faster than either of them were comfortable with. They needed to take a breath and regroup.

"I want to hear about all of it," he promised. "I'll really listen this time, too. I'm sorry about before."

"I know. It's okay."

It wasn't okay. It would be, though. For the first time in hours — really, the first time since they'd argued the previous night — he could breathe again.

It was more than relief. It was virtual nirvana. The rest would sort itself out. He had no doubt about that.

EIGHT

*T*hey spent the rest of the evening eating ... and talking. Once they broke the seal, they found it was much easier to relax around one another. Even though neither one of them could think beyond another kiss, they held it together and enjoyed each other's company. When it was time for Cooper to say goodbye, he forced himself to remain calm as she walked him to the door.

"I'm glad we've worked through this," she admitted as she hovered in front of the opening. "I didn't like fighting with you."

"I didn't like it either." His fingers were gentle as he slipped a strand of hair behind her ear. "Are you feeling okay?"

She nodded even though she was certain her heart might burst out of her chest given his proximity. "Are you?"

"I am. We need to talk more about the potential demon aspect tomorrow. For tonight, I think you should get some sleep."

"It's hard. I spend all my time tossing and turning, worrying."

"About being sued?"

"About all of it. Being sued ... the boy ... all of it."

"I can't tell you not to worry." He pulled closer. "It's going to be okay, though. I know that's hard for you to believe, but I want you to have faith. Can you at least try?"

She nodded. "I can try."

"Good." He leaned forward, and this time the kiss he pressed to her lips was soft and sweet. "Lock this door when I leave. I'll make sure the downstairs door is locked, too."

She sighed, amused. "You never let this security persona go, do you?"

"Not when there's something to keep safe." He gave her another peck and then stepped through the door, frowning when something glinted on the floor and caught his attention. "What's this?" He scooped up the item and held it up in the light, frowning when he realized what it was. "Is this a key? Where did it come from?"

Hannah forced her attention to the item in the palm of his hand. This time her heart skipped a beat for a different reason. "Where did you find that?"

"It was on the floor."

"But ... where did it come from?" She lifted her eyes and searched the area around the door. "I ... do you know what this is?" She almost looked excited as she grabbed the key, her eyes immediately going to the locked cabinet against the far wall.

Cooper followed her gaze, realization dawning. "That's the key to the cabinet."

"The cabinet I haven't been able to open since I moved here."

He grinned. It felt somehow kismet that two things had worked themselves out this evening, although he was still confused how the key had magically appeared. "Well, what are you waiting for? Open it."

Hannah had wanted nothing more — er, well, mostly nothing more — since she arrived in Casper Creek. Now that she had the opportunity, she found herself suddenly reticent. "Oh, well ... ."

As if reading her mind, Cooper nodded in understanding and closed her fingers over the key. "Take your time. When you're ready to open the cabinet, you'll know it."

She exhaled on a shaky breath, relieved that he understood what was holding her back without having to explain. Suddenly the pressure was on and she wasn't quite sure she wanted to deal with it at the same time she was dealing with everything else. "I just want to give it the night. You're right about me needing sleep."

"You're going to find that I'm always right."

She laughed, as he'd intended. "I'm glad you don't suffer from a weak ego. That would be boring."

"You don't ever have to worry about that with me." He gave her another kiss and then blew out a breath, rueful. "I need to get out of here. I'm just delaying the inevitable."

"I'll be fine," she reassured him. "You don't have to worry."

"As you've aptly pointed out, worrying comes with the business. I'll be back tomorrow morning. I'll bring breakfast for you and Tyler. With the park closed, it will just be the three of us. That will allow us time to bandy about some ideas, though."

Hannah nodded, excited at the prospect. "Okay, well, then I guess I will see you tomorrow."

"You definitely will." He winked as he slipped through the door.

Hannah locked it as soon as he disappeared and then turned to find Jinx staring at her from his place on the couch. His expression was accusatory.

"Oh, don't look at me like that," she chided. "It's just a ... flirtation. He's not replacing you. I promise."

Jinx didn't look convinced.

"Should we go to bed?"

The dog recognized the word and raced in the direction of the bedroom, causing her to laugh. He took up more than half the bed, but he was worth it.

Hannah squeezed the key in her hand and looked back to the cabinet, momentarily tempted. Then she shook her head. All things happened when they were meant to happen. She wasn't quite there yet ... and that was fine.

SHE TOOK EXTRA CARE WITH HER appearance the next morning, which made her feel shallow. That didn't stop her from putting on a light coat of makeup and dressing in flattering shorts that highlighted her long legs. She also pulled on her favorite T-shirt, which looked simple but showed off her assets to their full effect.

Cooper was just arriving in the saloon, a bag of food in his hand, when she descended the stairs. Jinx barreled past him when he offered a greeting, racing through the swinging saloon doors and heading outside without giving up as much of a sniff.

"Apparently he's over me, huh?" Cooper smirked as he shook his head, his heart rate picking up a notch when he got a full gander at Hannah. She looked ... great. There was no other word he could think to use. If he didn't know better, he would say that she was glowing. "Hey."

Hannah's nerves were back and they made her slightly jittery, something she internally admonished herself for as she settled at the table. "Hey."

They eyed each other for what felt like a long time. Cooper had just decided that it was time to turn the conversation to the elephant in the room when a cheerful whistle drew his attention to the doors. Tyler, freshly showered and clearly in a good mood, pushed his way into the room with Jinx on his heels.

"Good morning," he called out, taking a moment to greet Jinx with a hearty hug and stroking session. "Who's a good boy?"

"I am," Cooper replied, finally breaking eye contact with Hannah and taking the seat to her right. He was antsy being in such close proximity without being able to touch her, but he reminded himself that it would happen again — was destined to happen again really — and he should show some patience. "I brought breakfast."

"See. I knew you were good for something." Tyler beamed as he moved to sit at the table. "I take it you guys made up." When neither of them immediately commented, he turned his full attention on each of them for the first time since entering the saloon. Immediately, he caught the furtive glances they sent one another. "Oh, so you guys really made up, huh?" He broke into a wide grin. "Did you make up all the way or only part of the way?"

Cooper skewered him with a dark look. "I can't believe you just said that."

"Yeah, well, I'm a kid at heart." Tyler took the container of food Cooper handed to him. "Seriously, you guys must've had quite the night. Did you leave?"

Cooper wanted to shake his friend until he stopped uttering nonsense. "I didn't spend the night here. It's none of your business if I did, though. You need to ... chill."

"Definitely." Hannah appeared more amused at Tyler's antics than Cooper, although that was to be expected. "You should totally chill."

"Oh, you're so cute." Tyler gave her cheek a squeeze and laughed when Cooper glowered at him. "This is going to be so much fun. I can see that already."

"You're going to stay out of it," Cooper muttered, opening

his container and immediately reaching for a slice of toast. "There's no need to act like a juvenile."

"Says the guy who is sucking all the fun out of the room," Tyler shot back. "I'm going to focus all of my attention on Hannah this morning. She's prettier anyway. Tell me all the details."

Hannah was new to Casper Creek, but she'd become accustomed to Tyler's antics in a short amount of time. "Well ... we found the key to Abigail's cabinet."

Whatever he was expecting, that wasn't it. Tyler turned to Cooper with accusatory eyes. "That had better be a euphemism for something. If not, you and I are going to have a little talk about the birds and the bees. You clearly don't understand how this is supposed to work."

Hannah giggled, the sound warming Cooper's heart. He realized that he was more than happy to put up with a little ribbing from Tyler if it meant she would laugh that way for the rest of her life.

"It appeared out of nowhere," Cooper explained, slathering his toast with jelly. "I found it on the floor when I was leaving."

Tyler made a face. "And you don't know where it came from?"

"No." Cooper turned thoughtful as he chewed his toast, waiting until he swallowed to speak again. "I've been thinking about it, though. We kind of crashed into the doorframe a little bit. I think maybe the key was on top and we jarred it loose."

Tyler was back to being amused. "You crashed into the doorframe?"

Cooper turned stiff. "That's what I said."

"What were you doing when you crashed into the doorframe?"

"Don't worry about it."

85

Tyler wasn't about to let it go. Hannah and Cooper would be his sole source of entertainment for the day. He had every intention of milking them for everything they were worth. "Did you have your tongues down each other's throats at the time?"

"Don't answer that," Cooper warned, extending a plastic fork in Hannah's direction. "Don't dignify that with a response."

"You need to stop irritating him," Hannah chided, shaking her head as she dug into her omelet. Cooper had included everything she liked, hadn't missed a single item, and she found that little fact was enough to bolster her spirits. "What are we going to do all day if nobody is up here?"

"Maybe you can learn to ride a horse," Tyler suggested. "You've been putting it off since you arrived. Today might be the perfect day."

Hannah balked. "I know how to ride a horse."

"You said you rode a pony at the fair when you were a kid. That's not the same thing."

"Don't give her grief," Cooper instructed. "If she doesn't want to learn to ride, she doesn't have to. Not everyone rides a horse here."

The words stirred curiosity in Hannah. "Do you ride a horse?" she asked Cooper, genuinely curious.

"I can ride." He evaded her gaze. "Let's talk about demons."

Hannah had to press her lips together to keep from laughing out loud. When she risked a glance at Tyler, she found him equally amused. "Am I missing something?"

Tyler shook his head. "Cooper can ride. He wasn't lying about that. He just doesn't do it very often. He's never told me why. I think he might be afraid of the horses."

"I am not afraid of the horses," Cooper snapped. "Some of us just don't get the same thrill from riding a horse. Now, give me a snazzy Harley and an open highway and you'll see exactly how well I can ride." He winked at Hannah ... and then realized how filthy the unintended double entendre sounded. "Wait, that came out wrong."

Tyler laughed so hard he almost choked. Cooper had to slap his back to make sure his airway was clear.

"This really is going to be fun," he said once he was recovered. "I can't wait until the others find out."

On that note, Hannah had to disagree. She wasn't looking forward to that ... but it was a concern for another day.

AFTER BREAKFAST, COOPER BROKE from the group so he could spy on the state pathologist's people. He offered to take Hannah along for the ride, but she declined. She had no interest in watching them work.

Tyler took Jinx with him to the stables, which left Hannah at loose ends. With nothing else to do, she decided to look around the town and familiarize herself with the various businesses. So far, she'd spent the bulk of her time in the saloon. Eventually, she wanted to branch out.

When she first arrived in Casper Creek, she wasn't sure what to expect. In truth, she thought there was a chance she would eventually sell the property — maybe even to one of the workers — because she didn't think she would enjoy life away from the city. It turned out, she was wrong.

Sure, she'd only been here for a few weeks, but she'd already settled in. She was comfortable here, felt as if she belonged. She couldn't remember the last time she felt that way. She was starting to think it had never happened, which made what was occurring in Casper Creek a miracle.

Er, well, other than the unexplained death part. That pretty far from a miracle, but she was determined to figure out what was going on. She wouldn't let this hiccup derail her new life.

With that in mind, she let herself into the dry goods store and took stock of the layout. It wasn't a true representation of what a store would've looked like in the Old West. In fact, it was more of a tourist trap than anything. That didn't mean it wasn't appealing, though.

There were T-shirts, shot glasses, postcards, maps, and antique photographs. It was basically a souvenir hunter's paradise. The walls behind the cash register were filled with authentic items, and those were what she focused on now. She was determined to learn what she could about the store ... and then maybe take a shift in it as soon as the park was open again.

She was so lost in thought, fixated on what she was doing, she didn't hear the sound of shuffling feet on the hardwood floors until they were almost on top of her. Expecting Cooper — and perhaps looking forward to another kiss or two — she had a broad smile on her face when she turned. It evaporated almost immediately when she realized who was standing behind her.

"Patrick." The name came out in a gasp. The boy, who looked perfectly normal other than some disheveled hair, had somehow found himself at the top of the mountain ... even though it shouldn't have been possible. "What are you doing here?"

Despair flitted across the boy's features. He looked as if he were at the end of his rope. "My brother is missing."

It took Hannah a moment to absorb what he was saying. "Your brother is missing." She repeated the words and dusted her hands off on her shorts as she swiveled. "Logan? You're talking about Logan, right?"

Patrick looked exasperated. "I only have one brother."

"And you think he's here?" Hannah had no idea how to

respond. "I don't understand why you would think that. We're shut down for the day. We're not in operation. There's no way for him to get up here."

Something occurred to her. "Wait ... how did you get up here?"

"The same way we did the first time," Patrick snapped. "I rode the chairlift."

That made no sense to her. "But ... the chairlift isn't in operation today."

"Sure it is. How else do you think I got up here?"

Hannah felt completely out of her depth. She knew for a fact that the chairlift wasn't in operation. Ben, the operator, had the day off. The controls were locked. The chairlift most certainly wasn't in operation.

"But ... it's not working."

"That's how I got up here!" Patrick practically exploded, causing Hannah to take an inadvertent step back. Perhaps realizing how aggressive he was coming off, the boy immediately raised his hands in apology. "I'm sorry. I'm just ... afraid. I'm supposed to be watching him. He took off. My mother is going to be so upset."

Hannah's heart went out to him. "Why do you think he's here?"

"Because he was making noise about wanting to come back yesterday. My mother said that was never going to happen and to get over it. He got angry ... and then he was gone this morning."

"Well, then we'll just have to find him." She forced a smile for his benefit. "Do you know where he might be?"

"Why do you think I'm asking you for help?"

"I just thought maybe he might've liked a particular attraction when he was here before. I wasn't trying to upset you."

"Oh." Patrick turned sheepish. "I get what you're saying.

Yeah. He liked the saloon. My father said he couldn't go inside because it was full of drunks and he got mad because he couldn't look around like he wanted."

Hannah opted to ignore the "drunks" comment. The more she heard about Todd Lincoln, the more she disliked him. Now was not the time to dwell on that, though. "Then we'll head to the saloon." On instinct, she squeezed the boy's arm. "Don't worry. If he's up here, we'll find him."

"We have to. My mom can't take much more."

Hannah wordlessly nodded. She wasn't sure she could take much more either. She had a job to do, a responsibility to this place and the people who worked here, so she couldn't wallow. She had to be proactive, so that's exactly what she decided to be.

NINE

annah gripped Patrick's hand as they left the store. She didn't bother locking the door. She didn't have the time to worry. And, even though the boy was old enough that he should've been uncomfortable holding hands with a virtual stranger, he didn't give her any grief.

"Come on." Hannah gave him a firm tug and dragged him down the street. "We'll start at the saloon. If we can't find him, there are other people on the scene who might be able to help. I don't want you to panic."

Patrick didn't respond. The fear in his eyes, however, was enough to spur Hannah to move faster.

When they reached the saloon, she pushed through the door without hesitation. Unfortunately, the space was empty. She raced up the stairs long enough to check her apartment, but the door was locked and the boy obviously wasn't there.

Where could he have gone?

"I need you to stay here," she instructed Patrick when she rejoined him, grabbing him by the shoulders to make sure he was absorbing what she said. "If anyone else shows up — two men named Tyler or Cooper — tell them what's going on and that I'm out looking for Logan. Do you understand?"

Patrick's eyes filled with tears and his lower lip quivered. "You have to find him."

"I'm going to find him."

Hannah was determined when she left the saloon. She looked in both directions on Main Street. Finding nothing, she closed her eyes and opened her senses. She hadn't practiced the magic that seemed to be building inside of her, constantly clamoring for action, since she'd taken out Leanne. It wasn't that she was wallowing in guilt as much as she wanted to take a breather. She assumed she would have plenty of time to practice ... and now she was kicking herself for holding off. If there was ever a time she needed magic, it was now.

As if understanding her, the magic inside shifted into overdrive, and she turned with decided determination to the east as a small voice inside prodded her to move faster. She didn't question the voice, or the adrenaline rushing through her. Instead, she picked up her pace and started running.

It had been sunny earlier in the day. Only an hour before, in fact, the sun had been bright in the sky. Now it was overcast, cloudy, and there was a dreariness settling over the land. Hannah registered the weather phenomenon in the back of her mind but pushed it away to think about later. She had much more important things to focus on now.

The magic propelled her to the outskirts of town. She was on the far side, the area tucked away from view of Main Street. Tyler's stable was on the opposite side of town and Hannah was internally lambasting herself for not engaging his help before running off half-cocked. That thought completely dissipated, though, when she caught a hint of movement in the field behind the blacksmith station.

She pulled up short, her hands on her hips as she tried to

catch her breath, and frowned when she realized Logan was indeed there. The dark-haired boy was still, his gaze on the horizon, and he seemed lost in thought.

Hannah took a moment to watch him, curiosity getting the better of her. She hadn't forgotten his flashing eyes. She wasn't ready to discard the demon theory, which meant the boy could be dangerous. Now that she'd found him, the initial worry forgotten, she wanted to study him.

The compunction didn't last long.

It was the hissing sound, followed by a threatening rattle, that drew her attention. Her heart lodged in her throat as she took in the scene in its entirety. Logan was most definitely there, staring into nothing as if in a trance. Two feet in front of him had to be the largest snake Hannah had ever seen. It was coiled, tail shaking, and it looked ready to strike.

Hannah opened her mouth to warn Logan away. However, the words she thought she was going to say remained trapped inside. Instead, another word escaped, unbidden.

"*Glacio.*"

The word was foreign and yet Hannah knew what she was saying. As for the snake, it did as she instructed — in Latin, no less — and froze in its spot. Even as she marveled at what she'd managed to accomplish, Hannah rushed forward. She put herself between the boy and the serpent, which was probably unwise, and stared hard into his eyes.

He was most definitely in a trance, lost to the world, and the fear Hannah felt dissipate when the snake stopped moving reappeared with a vengeance.

What in the heck was going on here?

"I WANT HER ARRESTED RIGHT NOW!"

Lindsey was shrill when she arrived on top of the mountain. Her voice was screechy, her eyes sharp. She also looked as if she'd lost a few pounds and was on the verge of falling over because the weight of the world was so great it dragged at her diminutive shoulders.

Not long after tracking Hannah down, Cooper called Boone for backup. It was obvious he wanted to yell at her for taking off the way she did, but he managed to hold it together in front of witnesses ... just barely.

"And on what charges should I arrest her?" Boone asked calmly. Cooper had filled him in on the pertinent details mere seconds before Lindsey arrived. He was cool under pressure, though, and displayed none of the irritation he was obviously feeling.

Lindsey's eyes filled with fire. "She kidnapped my son!"

Cooper made a growling sound deep in his throat, but Boone shot him a quelling look that was enough to silence him. When Boone turned back to Lindsey, he had on his pragmatic face.

"How did she do that?" he queried. "She was here all morning. There are witnesses."

"Witnesses on her payroll."

"There are also cameras at the base of the mountain," Boone added. "I have men down there right now. Do you know what they told me? The cover has been pried off the chairlift controls. That means someone broke into the equipment from the bottom of the mountain. Why would Hannah do that when she has a vehicle?"

"I—" Lindsey broke off and worked her jaw. When she regrouped, she had a different plan of attack. "How did my son manage to get the cover off the controls?"

"We're not sure, although there's a crowbar and hammer down there, too," Boone replied. "Both tools have the initials T and L burned into the handles. I'm assuming they belong to your late husband."

Lindsey looked like a guppy as she opened and closed her mouth. She obviously didn't have an answer.

"Mrs. Lincoln, I understand you're under a great deal of stress," Boone hedged. "I can't imagine what you're dealing with. Your son is the one who caused damage to Ms. Hickok's property in this particular instance, though. She is not to blame for what happened."

Cooper stirred. "She also saved your son from a rattlesnake," he added. "She put herself in danger to make sure he was okay."

Lindsey's gaze turned accusatory. "And I suppose I should just thank her for saving my son."

"That would be the polite thing to do," Boone agreed. "You don't strike me as a woman in a polite frame of mind, however. I can guarantee that Ms. Hickok is not to blame for what happened here.

"In fact, if she wanted, she could press charges against you," he continued, not missing a beat when Hannah jerked up her head and glared at him. "Your son damaged her property. He's to blame for this, not her."

Lindsey made an obscene sputtering noise. "I can't believe you're blaming this on him. He's a child."

"A child who knew exactly what he was doing when he headed out this morning. Your other son chased him, knew exactly where to go. According to the security footage, he was a full thirty minutes behind the younger boy. How did he manage that if there was no pre-meditation?"

"I ... ." Lindsey clearly didn't have an answer. "What do you want me to say?" That didn't mean she was willing to apologize, or suddenly turn soft. "If you think this is going to stop me from suing her, you're dead wrong. I'm going to take everything she has."

Hannah swallowed hard at the woman's words but

managed to remain silent. Cooper wasn't feeling as magnanimous.

"Ma'am, I understand that you've suffered a terrible loss," he started, ignoring the way Boone shifted to stare. "I can't imagine what you're going through. What happened isn't Hannah's fault, though. She wasn't even there."

Lindsey was incensed. "Are you saying it was Todd's fault?"

"No." Cooper immediately started shaking his head. "I think something terrible happened, but it was out of everybody's control. Sometimes things just happen and there's no one to blame for that."

"You're just saying that because you don't want to lose your job," Lindsey spat. "Well, let me tell you something: When this place is mine, I'm going to fire all of you. I'm going to make sure that everyone who had a hand in my husband's death pays."

Cooper thought about pressing her further but knew it was a wasted effort. The woman was clearly out of her mind with grief. She couldn't see past the future she believed she'd lost and recognize there were two boys who needed her love and attention. She was too bitter to focus on anybody but herself. To his utter surprise, it was Patrick who stepped in to smooth things over.

"Mom, you can't be mad at Ms. Hickok," he started, bracing himself with a steadying breath when her hateful glare landed on him. "I know you're sad about Dad — we're all sad and upset — but she didn't do this. When I went to her for help, she jumped right in. She made sure I was safe and then she went looking for Logan herself. She didn't even slow down for a second."

Lindsey held her oldest son's gaze for an extended beat, to the point where Hannah managed to convince herself that she was about to apologize ... or at least take a breath.

Instead, the bereaved woman started fervently shaking her head.

"Your father is dead. Do you know what that means? It means he's never going to another soccer game ... or baseball game ... or another picnic in the park." She started sobbing between words. "He's never going to be there to tuck you in or listen when you have a story. He won't be there for your children. He was stolen from us."

"Or perhaps he was accidentally lost," Boone countered. "Not everything terrible that happens is for malicious reasons."

"Oh, well, I can see where you stand on all of this." Lindsey collected herself quickly and grabbed Logan — who had remained absolutely silent since waking up in the field — by the shoulder. "We're going home. The next time you see us, it will be in court."

Hannah didn't say anything. Honestly, there was nothing to say. Until Lindsey started thinking clearly, it was impossible to have a conversation with the woman. Instead of pushing matters in a fruitless effort, Hannah focused on Patrick.

"Thank you for standing up for me," she offered in a low voice. "Thank you for coming after your brother, too. You were brave. If I hadn't known to start looking for him, something terrible could've happened. You were courageous and smart today. Good job."

Patrick nodded, morose. "I'm sorry."

"It's okay."

Lindsey grabbed her oldest child's arm and dragged him toward the door. "Don't apologize to her! We're suing her."

"Mom," Patrick sounded exasperated. "Just ... let it go."

"I will never let it go."

Hannah watched the small family shuffle toward the door, her eyes automatically going to Logan. She expected to

97

find the same vacant expression. Instead, the red eyes were back ... and he looked absolutely merciless.

A small gasp eked out of her mouth at the same moment a pile of evil energy invaded her mind with the strength of a wayward freight train. She took an inadvertent step back and almost fell over. Cooper was there to catch her, though, and he held her close as she sank to the floor.

Her senses were overloading, her mind threatening to collapse. Something very bad was happening, something terrible in origin. She didn't know how to fight it. All she could think as Lindsey disappeared with her children, none the wiser, was that her lights were about to go out permanently.

The pain was so great she almost welcomed it.

HANNAH FELT AS IF SHE'D BEEN run over by a semi-truck when she woke. She was on her couch, a blanket resting over her, and when she shifted her eyes to the left she found Cooper sitting on a chair watching her.

"Hey." Her voice sounded ragged, as if she'd been gargling razor blades all day.

"Hey." His face was filled with concern as he leaned forward. "How are you feeling?"

To Hannah, that was a complicated question. "I've felt better. What happened?"

"I was just about to ask you that. What do you remember?"

Hannah struggled to prop herself up so she was no longer prone on the couch. "I remember being in the saloon. Lindsey Lincoln was there ... the boys ... she was extremely angry."

"She had no right to talk to you the way she did."

"I don't know that I feel that way. If it was my kid … ." She didn't finish the sentence. She didn't have to.

Cooper reached over and snagged her hand, giving it a firm squeeze. "You didn't cause any of this, Hannah. You were minding your own business, trying to learn the ropes up here, and this happened to you. It didn't happen because of you."

He was so earnest Hannah could do nothing but sigh. "Thanks for saying that. It's nice having you in my corner."

She didn't expand on the statement, but Cooper recognized the part she left off. "You were going to add 'for a change,' weren't you?"

"No."

"Yes, you were."

"No, I wasn't."

"Don't deny it."

All she could do was sigh. "Do you really have to pick a fight when I'm not feeling my best?"

He laughed at her expression, which was somewhere between annoyance and mirth. "I'm sorry." He lifted her hand and pressed a kiss to the palm, which was romantic enough to cause her heart to stutter and corny enough to cause her to grin. "What happened to you there at the end? It almost looked as if you were having a seizure."

Being reminded of the magical assault was enough to wipe the smile off her face. "I saw it again." She swallowed hard. "The eyes. The red eyes. I saw them again."

Concerned, Cooper shifted from the chair to the couch, sliding her legs over so he could get comfortable next to her. His arm automatically went around her shoulders and he tucked her in tight at his side.

"I was watching the kid a lot of the time," he admitted, smoothing her hair. "You're right about him being off. None of his reactions were normal. I didn't see red eyes, though. When did you see them?"

"When they were walking out. He kind of looked back, over his shoulder, and he stared directly at me."

"I was focused on Lindsey when they were leaving. Maybe a little on Patrick, too. I feel bad for that kid. He's suddenly the man of the house and he's chafing under the additional weight."

"Yeah." Hannah rested her hand on Cooper's chest and closed her eyes. "Either the kid is evil or there's something evil inside of the kid."

"Tell me about the snake. You didn't have a lot of time before. I should've asked more questions, but I assumed it was a normal encounter. I'm guessing there was more to it than that."

Hannah bobbed her head. "There was definitely more to it than that. It was as if he was frozen. I mean ... he wasn't moving. He was staring into nothing and the snake was coiled and about to strike. He didn't do a thing to get away from it."

"But you did. You did something to the snake, right?"

"Yeah. Actually ... I'm still not sure what I did. It was like when Leanne came after me. I just reacted. Something inside of me knew exactly what to do."

"That's because you're awesome." He kissed her forehead and grinned when she rolled her eyes. "What? Too much?"

"Just a little bit."

"I'm sorry. I'll try to be a little less schmaltzy."

"I don't mind the schmaltz. It's kind of sweet."

"That's me. Kind of sweet."

"You're entirely sweet when you want to be."

"Don't tell anyone. I want to maintain my street cred."

"I'll try to refrain." She closed her eyes again and let loose a small sigh. "I didn't know rattlers were in Kentucky. It was kind of a surprise."

"They're here, although they're nowhere near as prevalent as other places ... like Texas. Most of the time you never see them. They hang by Mammoth Cave. I don't know why this one was up here."

"Maybe it was here for the boy."

Cooper stilled. "You think the snake attacked him because it recognized he was different?"

"I don't know. It's something to think about, though."

"It definitely is."

They lapsed into amiable silence that was only interrupted by a knock on the door. Then, not waiting for anyone to answer, Tyler barreled through with takeout bags in his hands. He stopped when he saw them on the couch.

"Is this a private moment or can anyone join in?"

Cooper glared at him. "It's a private moment."

"Don't be hasty," Hannah interjected, a mischievous smile on her face. "I might be open to suggestions depending on what's in those bags."

Tyler barked out a laugh at Cooper's sour expression. "I knew this was going to be fun."

Cooper wanted to argue the point but Hannah's laughter had him rethinking his stance. There were worse things than sharing a meal with Tyler, after all. He was up for whatever bolstered her spirits.

TEN

*I*t turned out, Tyler was a witty conversationalist. He had Hannah laughing until her already hoarse voice was ragged.

Cooper spent his time making sure she didn't overexert herself while keeping her flush with fluids and joining in on the occasional story. In truth, he wasn't as gregarious as Tyler. That didn't stop Hannah from sticking close to him, absorbing his warmth as she recovered, and looking to him constantly to make sure he was enjoying himself.

It was an entertaining evening.

"Well, I think I should probably get out of your hair," Tyler offered, glancing at the clock shortly before seven. "It's getting late and you guys probably want some alone time to finish up whatever it is you were starting when I came with dinner."

"You don't have to go," Hannah protested automatically.

"Yes, he does," Cooper countered sternly, earning a hearty chuckle from Tyler.

Hannah elbowed him in the stomach before climbing to

shaky feet and walking Tyler to the door. "Thanks so much for dinner ... and the stories."

"Don't worry about it." Tyler squeezed her shoulder and slid his gaze to Cooper. "Are you spending the night?"

Even though he didn't consider himself the sort to be embarrassed, Cooper's cheeks heated as he shot his friend a death glare. "No. I'll be staying long enough to make sure Hannah is comfortable. Don't go spreading that rumor."

"Definitely not," Hannah agreed, although she seemed more amused at the prospect than Cooper. "I don't want to earn a reputation for being the loosest bar wench in the Old West."

Tyler laughed, delighted, and then gave her an impulsive hug. "I'm glad you're okay. I still don't know what happened, but I'm going to leave you with Doc Wyatt here and I'm sure you'll be feeling up to snuff tomorrow."

Hannah returned the embrace. "I'm sure you're right."

Once it was just the two of them, she turned back to Cooper and discovered his cheeks were still burning with color. She found his reaction adorable ... and a bit ridiculous. "Are you embarrassed because you don't want people to find out we're together?"

He straightened. "No. Why would you possibly think that?"

She shrugged and held out her hands. "I don't know. You just seem ... unhappy. Yeah, that's the word I would use. If you want to change your mind about what happened last night, I get it. You don't have to suffer through this if you don't want to."

He took two long strides and loosely gripped her wrists, bringing them up to hold against his chest. "I haven't changed my mind. Don't think that."

She turned sheepish. "I just want to make sure."

"Well, you can rest assured that I'm exactly where I want

to be." He smiled because she was the one suffering from a mild case of discomfort this time. "Actually, I would prefer being over there, but I'm flexible." He gestured toward the couch, which was enough to have Hannah grinning again.

"I think that can be arranged."

They settled on the couch, Cooper snagging the blanket she'd discarded earlier and placing it on her lap. Jinx, who had fallen asleep when he realized no one was going to share their dinner with him, perked up long enough to move from the floor to the couch and then he crashed out again.

So, there they were. The chief of security, a new witch who was magically attacked earlier in the day, and everyone's favorite canine friend.

"Tell me what you were feeling when you went down in the saloon," Cooper prodded, his hand moving to Hannah's neck so he could rub at the tension pooling there. "I'm curious exactly what that kid threw at you."

"I honestly don't know that I can explain it. One second I was fine. The next ... well, the next his eyes turned red and it felt as if someone was twisting my brain. You know when you're a kid and you do those burn things to each other's arms? Like ... you use one hand to twist one way and the other to twist another?"

He nodded wordlessly.

"It felt like that was being done to my brain. It hurt. Like ... literally hurt. It wasn't just that I was being overpowered. I was being assaulted over and over. When I finally passed out I welcomed it because it meant an end to the pain."

"I'm sorry." He kissed her temple and continued rubbing. "From where I was standing, it almost looked as if you fainted. I thought maybe you got lightheaded because of the threats Lindsey was throwing around."

"That wasn't a highlight of my day, but I don't usually get lightheaded."

"Good to know."

"Besides, she was already out the door when Logan attacked. She didn't even see what was happening."

"I noticed that, too. I was also grateful for it. I didn't want to give her ammunition against you, and while I don't think fainting is an actionable offense, it's better that she doesn't know ... at least right now."

"Yeah." Hannah rubbed her forehead. She didn't have a headache, but fatigue was starting to set in. Still, she didn't want to be alone. Or, perhaps she simply wasn't ready for him to call it a night. That was a possibility, too. "I've been thinking of opening the cabinet."

The words were out before she realized she was going to utter them.

"Really?" Cooper cocked an eyebrow. "I figured you might wait until this was over. I thought for sure you would have it open before I left last night. Then, when you hesitated, I realized you weren't ready. What changed your mind?"

"A couple of things. Seeing Astra, for one."

He frowned. "I talked to her after you left. She said she wasn't mean to you."

"I think that's a matter of perspective. It's not important, though. She was helpful in the fact that she said she was going to research demons. I'm assuming that means she has books she can tap, right?"

He nodded. "She has an extensive library."

"Did Abigail have an extensive library?"

He caught up to where she was going. "You think that Abigail's books are in that cabinet and you want to see if she has any research materials on demons."

"Do you think that's stupid?"

"No. I think it's smart. I also think you're nervous about what else you might find in that cabinet."

"Maybe a little. Is *that* stupid?"

He chuckled at her adorable expression. "No." He kissed the corner of her mouth and turned his full attention to the cabinet. "I don't want to overstep my bounds here — so just tell me if I'm out of line — but maybe you would feel more comfortable if I was with you when you opened the cabinet."

Hannah didn't realize she was holding her breath until it whooshed out. "Would you?"

"I was gung-ho to open it last night. I'm totally in."

"My mind was too fuzzy to open it last night."

"Are you saying I fuzzed your brain? I think that's the nicest thing you've ever said to me."

"Once I'm feeling a hundred percent again, I'll think of something else that's nice to say," she promised.

COOPER HUNG CLOSE AS SHE RETRIEVED the key from her bedroom — she'd taken over the guest room rather than the main room because she didn't feel right invading Abigail's space. Since her ghost was still hanging around — although not of late — that seemed like a wise decision ... at least for the foreseeable future.

"Here we go." She inserted the key in the lock and let loose a breath when she heard it click. Her first attempt at lifting the top on the cabinet was a failure because it was so heavy. Cooper pitched in the second time, though, and it easily opened.

Inside was a virtual cornucopia of items, most of which Hannah had no idea what to make of.

"What's this?" She pulled out a crystal pendant. It was attached to a piece of leather. "It's not big enough to be a necklace."

He chuckled at her confused expression. "That is a scrying stone."

Her face remained blank. "What's a scrying stone?"

"It's kind of like a magical GPS device." He scratched his chin as he searched for the best way to explain things to her. "Once when one of the horses went missing, Abigail got out a map of the area and used that stone to find the horse."

"How?"

"I don't know. She kind of swung it around and then it dropped to the right spot. I was doubtful, but when I headed out I found the horse. He'd been spooked by something and Tyler had to coax him home. The scrying worked like a charm, though."

"Huh." Hannah stared at the stone for another minute and then set it aside. She would practice being a magical GPS later. "What's this?" She pulled out an Ouija board and held it up under the light.

"You can't be serious. You don't know what that is?"

"It looks like an Ouija board."

"It is an Ouija board."

"Why would Abigail have a Ouija board?"

He shrugged. "I think she talked to ghosts on it."

"Why wouldn't she just talk to them like I talk to her?"

"It's my understanding that it's difficult for ghosts to take corporeal shape. I mean ... when was the last time you saw Abigail? I don't think it's easy for her to manifest."

"I've been wondering about that." Hannah lowered the board to the floor and carefully tucked it out of sight. "I thought maybe she lost interest in talking to me."

"I very much doubt that's true. She talked about you ... a lot. I'm guessing she's gathering her power. Didn't she mention that she was having trouble controlling her new reality?"

"Yeah. It's been almost two weeks, though."

"Well, have you talked to Jackie about it?"

Hannah pressed her lips together and shook her head.

"May I ask why not?" he prodded.

"Well ... after I killed Leanne, I kind of wanted to put some distance between the magic and me. It's not that I want to ignore it — I don't think it's going to allow me to do that regardless — but I wanted some time to think about it."

"And that meant keeping your distance from Jackie and the other coven members," he deduced. "I get it. That was probably a good idea. The thing is, Jackie is going to be able to better answer your questions than me. I'm kind of an outsider when it comes to witch stuff. Jackie is an actual participant ... and she's smart. You can trust her."

"Yeah." Hannah reached into the cabinet and pulled out an aged book. It looked to be made of leather and was so well worn that the corners were no longer smooth. "Here we go. Do you think there's anything about demons in here?"

Cooper gave her a sidelong look. "I don't know. I think that's Abigail's grimoire."

Hannah felt as if she was in the middle of a college examination and yet she'd missed every class before the mid-term. "What's a grimoire?"

"It's a magic book. Like a magic diary. It's where Abigail kept track of her spells, jotted down ingredients for potions, that sort of thing."

Hannah worked her jaw. "So ... this is like her most personal belonging."

"Yeah. I guess that's fair to say."

Hannah was reverent as she flipped the book over, her fingers grazing the snap that kept the book locked tight. "Do you think I should open this?"

"Do you want to open it?"

That was a difficult question for Hannah to answer. "Yeah. It feels somehow rude, though."

"Abigail left everything to you. That includes this book. If she didn't want you to open it, she would've said something.

"The thing is, Abigail was the sort of person who loved

having a student," he continued. "Before Astra turned on her, she thrived at being a teacher. I think she wants to be your teacher ... just as soon as she gets a handle on being a ghost, that is."

"So ... I should open it. That's what you're saying, right?"

"Do you want my permission?"

"I just don't want to do the wrong thing."

"You're not going to do the wrong thing." Here was where Hannah's low self-esteem — which he had no doubt came from what happened with her ex-boyfriend — became frustrating. "If you want to be a good witch, you need to get over the fear."

Wordlessly, Hannah nodded. Her finger shook a bit as she opened the hasp on the journal. She only hesitated for a second before flipping open the book. Then, like some magical fairy show, a pile of sparkly magic dust floated from the pages and began twirling over her head. She gasped as it danced, her eyes lighting up.

Cooper watched, flabbergasted, as the dust kept a beat and rhythm. It moved faster as it circled higher. He realized what was going to happen a second before the dust slammed into Hannah's chest, knocking her sideways.

"Hannah!" He reached for the book, every intention of grabbing it from her hands, but instead of going down thanks to the magical assault, Hannah laughed. That's when he realized her voice was back to normal. She was no longer hoarse. Her color was back, too. It was as if the grimoire understood she was weak and struggling and decided to give her an extra boost.

That didn't mean he was ready to give up worrying. "Are you okay?" He drew her into his arms and stared into her sea-blue eyes. He was ready to throw her over his shoulder and drive her to the doctor himself if he saw the slightest hint that she was struggling.

"I feel ... good," she said after a moment, bewildered. "What just happened?"

"I have no idea. It was pretty cool, though."

"It definitely was." Hannah let loose a laugh that was gay enough to cause his heart to skip a beat. "Do you think magic is always like that? Fun, I mean."

"Probably not. You've witnessed some magic that was the exact opposite of fun."

"True. I'm still glad I saw this. I feel better."

He returned her smile. "That's good. I always want you to feel better."

"Should we keep looking?"

"I don't have any other plans tonight."

IT WAS ALMOST MIDNIGHT BEFORE Cooper left. Hannah considered inviting him to stay in the apartment — on the couch, of course — but ultimately she lost her nerve. It was too soon for them to be entertaining that thought. That didn't mean they didn't engage in a heckuva make-out session before separating.

Once he left, however, Hannah made sure to return the grimoire to the cabinet — she didn't want to risk losing it so soon after she found it — and then coaxed a reticent Jinx into the bedroom. She was out two minutes after her head hit the pillow, and thanks to the dose of magic from the grimoire, her dreams were nothing but pleasant.

That's why she was confused when she bolted to a sitting position three hours later. She'd been mired in a ridiculously fun dream, one where Cooper took her on a picnic by the creek and absolutely no one interrupted them. She wanted to return to that dream, but her anxiety kicked up a notch, to the point where she was convinced there was something wrong.

Her first thought was Jinx, but he was sound asleep in the bed beside her. He didn't have a care in the world. In fact, he didn't stir when she climbed out of bed and made her way into the living room.

She wasn't sure what drew her there. Something inside pointed her in that direction, though, and she stood in the hallway staring at the empty room for what felt like forever. Nothing moved. Nothing was out of place. There was simply ... nothing.

She'd just about made up her mind to turn on her heel and go to bed when she saw the curtains by the window flutter. It took her a moment to remember the window wasn't open, so there should be no reason for the curtains to move. It wasn't as if there was a cross-breeze.

"Who's there?" Hannah's voice came out squeaky, the fear overtaking her.

Then, as if straight from a dream, two eyes flashed in the darkness. They were red ... and unattached to a corporeal body. The moon was full enough that it cast a pall over the room. She could see hints of movement, and whatever shape went with the eyes wasn't solid but rather a shadow.

It was a ghost ... or something akin to a ghost.

"Abigail?" Hannah's hand shook as it flew to her mouth. She wanted to flee, run anywhere else, but she was rooted to her spot.

The eyes held hers for a long beat ... and then they melted into the curtains as the specter fell through the wall and disappeared from the apartment.

Hannah should've felt better. She should've been relieved. Her heart wouldn't stop pounding, though. The fear wouldn't recede.

So she stood there, frozen so long her legs practically gave out. That's when she finally returned to her bedroom.

Sleep was elusive, though. She couldn't push the sight out of her head and her mind was busy with possibilities.

What was the thing in the living room? Did it come from the grimoire? Did the demon inside Logan send it? Was it the demon detached from his body? Or, was it something else entirely? Perhaps Astra sent whatever it was to try to get the grimoire. Anything was possible.

Finally, when the sun started to lift above the horizon, Hannah managed to close her eyes again. She wouldn't be able to get much sleep but a little was better than nothing.

At least that's what she told herself.

ELEVEN

*H*annah was hollow-eyed and slow-moving when she hit the main floor of the saloon. Tyler and Cooper already had breakfast spread out when she appeared, and were talking about some golf outing they participated in every year.

Cooper was instantly alert. "What happened?" He strode toward her and pressed his hand to her forehead without invitation. "Are you sick? I think it's time we take you to the hospital."

Hannah arched an eyebrow. "And good morning to you, too."

Cooper ignored the sarcasm. "I wanted to take you to the hospital yesterday, but Tyler and Boone said it was a bad idea because people might ask questions and then there would be a medical record that Lindsey could use against us. I no longer care what they say. You're going to the hospital."

Hannah merely waved off his concern. "I'm not sick. I just didn't sleep well."

"You're so pale I can practically see through you," he shot back. "You looked good when I left."

"At midnight," Tyler offered, smirking when Cooper pinned him with a dark look. "What? I wasn't spying or anything. I just happened to hear your truck in the parking lot when you took off. That's not on me. You should drive quieter if you want to be stealthy."

"Oh, shut it." Cooper stroked his hand down the back of Hannah's head. On a normal day, she pulled her hair back in a cute bun so she could show off her shoulders in her saloon uniform. Today, her hair was loose and free. The shadows under her eyes bothered him more than anything.

"I think you should sit down." He led her toward a chair and made sure she was comfortable before rummaging in the takeout bag he'd brought with him. "Here. I got some juice."

Hannah stared at the bottle he shook. "I don't need juice."

"Don't you like orange juice?"

"It's fine."

"Then I think you should drink it."

"Yes, juice is magical," Tyler intoned, ignoring the glare Cooper lobbed in his direction. "Juice will make everything okay. It's a magical elixir."

"Shut up." Cooper elbowed his friend but kept his eyes on Hannah. "I really don't like how pale you are."

"Well, I'm sorry about that." Hannah chose her words carefully. "I don't want to worry you. I'm not sick, though. That's not what this is."

"Okay." Cooper feigned patience. "Tell me what this is."

"Something happened last night."

"I knew it." Tyler looked practically triumphant, a wide smile on his face. After a few seconds, the smile faltered. "Wait ... if something happened between the two of you, why did Cooper leave in the middle of the night?" His gaze turned accusatory. "You can't just leave after. That makes you a dog."

Cooper's glare was withering. "Stop being annoying!"

"Stop yelling," Hannah muttered, rubbing her forehead. "I have a headache."

"See." Now it was Cooper's turn to puff out his chest. "She's sick. She needs to go to the hospital."

"I'm not sick." Hannah slapped away his hand when he reached for her forehead a second time. "I don't have a fever. Physically, I'm fine."

Tyler caught on to what she wasn't saying before Cooper. "What about mentally? What did you guys do last night?"

"That's none of your business," Cooper muttered.

Hannah agreed it was none of his business, but she wanted an opinion from both men. "We finally got the cabinet open." Her voice was low. "There was a lot of stuff inside."

Tyler slid his eyes to Cooper, an unsaid question drifting across his features.

"I was there for that," Cooper confirmed. "Nothing happened, though." Then, unbidden, an image of the dust rising from the book and smacking into her chest assailed him. "Well, almost nothing." He licked his lips and moved his hand to the back of Hannah's neck so he could rub. "Maybe we should call for Jackie. She might be able to tell us more about that magic book thing."

Hannah wasn't opposed to that. Still, it wasn't her main worry. "It wasn't what happened with the grimoire. I definitely want to talk to Jackie about that, but ... that's not why I didn't sleep."

"If you won't go to the hospital, maybe we can get a doctor to come out here." Cooper was officially fixated on her health and wouldn't let it go. "You can sit down — or, better yet, I'll carry you upstairs and you can lie down — and I'll get someone out here to check on you."

Hannah's eyes darkened as she drew her eyebrows together. "Cooper, I know you're trying to help — no, really I do — but if you mention the hospital one more time, I'm going to strangle you."

"And she won't have sex with you," Tyler added helpfully.

Hannah moved her annoyed glare to the veterinarian. "Tyler, if you don't stop making inappropriate sexual jokes to irritate Cooper, I'm going to strangle you, too."

He had the grace to be abashed. "I didn't mean to embarrass you."

"I'm not embarrassed. Another morning I would've found it funny. Something legitimately happened last night, though."

For the first time since she descended the stairs and Cooper went off on a tangent about her health, he really looked at her. More importantly, he listened. "What is it? What happened? Was it Astra?"

"I honestly don't know." Hannah sucked in a breath to steady herself. "So, the thing is, after you left last night I crashed out hard. Basically I locked the apartment door, put the grimoire back in the cabinet and locked it because I didn't think it was wise to leave it out in the open, and then crawled into bed. I was out fast and was in the middle of a great dream when something woke me."

This time when Cooper tensed it was for a different reason. "What happened?"

"I don't know. I might've heard something, but I don't know that I believe that because Jinx never stirred. He was down for the count and that's why I headed into the living room by myself. I figured if someone was inside, he would've woken up."

Cooper's heart sank. "Someone was in your apartment?" He jerked up his chin and stared at the second floor. "I'll switch every lock in this town tonight. I'll buy an electrical security system, too. I won't leave until you feel safe again."

Tyler shot his friend a dubious look. "Dude, I don't think she's done with her story."

"I'm not," Hannah agreed. "Thank you, Tyler. I'm glad one of you is taking the time to listen to me."

Tyler preened under the compliment. "You're welcome."

"Oh, don't get too full of yourself," Cooper chided. "You're the one who was one building over and didn't know she was in trouble."

Tyler's smile faltered. "I didn't think of that. I'm so sorry, Hannah."

Now her temper did flare and she slammed her hands on the table to get their attention. "I know you guys are alpha males and you like to take control of a conversation, but I have a serious problem. If you guys aren't willing to listen to me, I'll take my concerns someplace else."

Cooper's eyes turned dark. "We're listening."

"No, you're not. My story isn't even that long, but I can't get it out because you guys keep interrupting."

Cooper wanted to argue but the more he thought about it, the more he realized she was right. She'd barely said anything. Every notion he'd run with had come from his head. He felt ashamed.

"I'm sorry, darling," he offered lamely. "I didn't mean to ... tell me what happened." He straightened and regrouped. "Tell me it from start to finish."

Gratified — and a little flustered at the "darling" endearment — Hannah slid into one of the open chairs. "There was something in the living room when I went out there. The curtains moved. For a second, I thought I left the window open. I knew that wasn't the case, though."

"No, I definitely shut the windows," Cooper agreed. "I double-checked they were locked while you were sleeping." When he realized she was glaring at him, he held up his hands in capitulation. "I wasn't trying to interrupt that time. I was just trying to confirm."

Hannah rolled her eyes but remained calm. "I was frozen in place when I saw it."

"Saw what?" Tyler asked curiously. "I assume we're not talking about a normal invader, right?"

"Definitely not." Hannah wasn't sure about much, but she was definitely sure of that. "I thought it was a ghost at first. It was the eyes that told me differently, though."

Cooper was behind. "I don't understand."

"It was dark in the living room. I couldn't see. Then ... then there were these eyes. They glowed red. When the creature moved — and, no, I don't know what it was — it had a shadow for a body. It wasn't like when I saw Abigail. It wasn't like a regular ghost."

Cooper swallowed hard. "Did it touch you?"

She shook her head. "It looked at me. I think it was smiling. Then it disappeared through the wall — I mean ... like really disappeared into thin air — and I just stood there like an idiot."

"Did it come back?" Tyler asked.

"No."

"Did it say anything to you?"

"No."

Cooper's silence felt belligerent.

Slowly, she turned and found him scowling. "What? You can't possibly be mad at me. You're the one who kept interrupting."

"Oh, I'm mad at you." Cooper shook his head, disgusted. "I'm so mad at you I don't even know where to start."

"I'm the innocent victim here."

"You're most definitely innocent," he agreed. "You were also vulnerable ... and there was something in your apartment. Why didn't you call me?"

Hannah was taken aback. Honestly, she hadn't even considered it. "I don't know. I didn't want to bother you."

"You didn't want to bother me?" Cooper's eyes flashed with fury. "I'm head of security. You're supposed to bother me."

"Yeah, well ... I'm not weak."

"It's not about being weak. It's about being safe." He adjusted his tone because he could tell she was preparing to dig her heels in and fight. "I don't want anything to happen to you. It would upset me a great deal."

"Me, too," Tyler echoed, drawing Hannah's attention to him. "I get why you didn't want to bother Cooper. I get it better than he does. In your head, you probably thought he would assume you were calling him to come back because you changed your mind about sexy time."

Hannah's cheeks heated. "That didn't even cross my mind. I wasn't even thinking anything like that."

"Don't be an imbecile," Cooper snapped, hunkering down so he was at eye level with Hannah and softly moving her hair away from her face. He felt like a failure. "You should've called me. Did you think I wouldn't have dropped everything to get back to you?"

"I knew you would do exactly that," she countered. "I don't want you to see me as weak."

"Hannah, I could never see you as weak. You're too strong for anyone to see you as anything other than a strong woman. I promise you that."

Hannah was gratified by the words. "Thank you."

"You're welcome. I'm still kind of mad. You should've called me."

"She should've called me," Tyler corrected. "I was the one right across the way. Why didn't you come to me for help?"

That was a good question and Hannah was worried her answer would sound ridiculous. "I don't know," she admitted after a beat. "I just kind of stood there ... for hours. I was afraid to move, afraid it would come back. I couldn't even close my eyes again until it was light out."

Cooper's heart rolled, slow and painful. He hated thinking about her being terrified in such a manner. "Well, it's done now." He rubbed his thumb over her cheek and considered their options. "I think we need to talk to Jackie. She might know what it is that Hannah saw."

Hannah was already convinced she saw a demon, but she didn't want to start a fight if it wasn't necessary. "Let's call Jackie. That's an awesome idea."

UNLIKE THE MEN, JACKIE CAME in with no preconceived notions, listened to Hannah from beginning to end, and didn't interrupt once.

"It sounds like a demon," she announced when Hannah was finished with her tale.

Hannah swung her eyes to a worried-looking Cooper, and bit her lip to keep from hopping up and down in victory. The last thing she wanted was to argue with him ... again.

As if sensing her unease, Cooper squeezed her shoulder and nodded. "Fine. It was a demon."

Hannah exhaled heavily. "You believe me."

"Stop saying that." He swiveled on her. "I never didn't believe you. We've been over this a hundred times now. I believed you saw ... something. I was just confused about the demon part. I didn't think they were real."

"Oh, they're definitely real." Jackie was thoughtful as she stared out at the street. "I'm of two thoughts on this. The first is that the demon somehow manages to leave the boy at night and then return in the morning. Demons can't walk during the day without a physical shell."

"But they can walk at night without a shell?" Hannah queried.

"That's the rumor. I've never actually come face to face with a demon."

"Then how do we know we're dealing with a demon?" Cooper challenged. "I mean ... it could be something else, right? What if the thing Hannah saw isn't even tied to Logan? It could be something else entirely."

Hannah was frustrated. "What? What else could it possibly be?" She was sick of him questioning her and her temper was about to make a loud appearance.

"What if it's Astra?"

Hannah wasn't expecting the question. "Why would it be Astra?"

"Why does she do anything?" he grumbled. "I don't know why she would choose to attack this way ... other than the fact that you were down at the creek talking to her about demons yesterday. Maybe she decided to make a fake demon to scare you."

"In that case, her plan would've seemed to have worked," Tyler noted.

Hannah rubbed her cheek as she considered the suggestion. To be honest, it made sense. Astra was the sort of person who looked for a weakness to exploit at all times. Perhaps that's exactly what she tried to do with Hannah.

"I guess it's possible," she conceded after a few beats. "I don't really want to think that she's capable of doing something so heinous, but I've already seen her in action. She would do that and more to scare me away."

"She would," Cooper agreed. "It's possible Astra is behind this. It's also possible it's the thing inside the boy. I think we all agree there is something off about that kid."

"I only spent a few minutes with him yesterday, but I could tell that he wasn't a normal boy," Tyler agreed. "Not only does he show no outward signs of grieving, but he also has control over the mother and brother that no normal kid would be able to wield."

Cooper was surprised by the observation. "What do you mean?"

"I mean that the brother especially seemed afraid of him," Tyler replied, not missing a beat. "Patrick is older ... and bigger ... but there's real fear there. As for the mother, she never even really looked at the kid. She treats him like a commodity rather than a child."

"Did she look at Patrick?" Hannah asked.

"She did a few times. They seem to be relatively close. There's a wall between her and the other boy, though. It's obvious she feels she has a duty to take care of the kid because she's his mother, but she doesn't love him like she does Patrick."

Hannah tapped her foot on the ground. "I think we have to talk to Logan again. His mother can't be present for it either. It would be better if the brother was conveniently absent, too, quite frankly."

"Do you have a suggestion for how we get a child away from his grieving mother to question him about the demon living inside of him?" Tyler queried. "If so, I'm all ears."

"I do not have a suggestion." Hannah flicked her eyes to Cooper, hopeful. "He's the security guru. He's the one who should come up with the idea."

"I have an idea," Cooper confirmed, causing Hannah to brighten. "It's not one you're going to like, though."

Instantly, Hannah was suspicious. "You're going to cut me out of this, aren't you?"

Cooper knew better than lying. "Just this part of it," he reassured her quickly. "I'm going to need Boone to pull this off and we're going to have to head back to the house. If you're there, Lindsey will go off. She won't even consider leaving us alone with Logan. It's going to be hard enough to manipulate the situation without you, but it will be impossible if we have you in tow."

Hannah couldn't hide her disappointment. "But ... what if he only shows his demon side while I'm in the room?"

"Then we'll have to tackle that problem after the fact. For now, it's got to be Boone and me. It's the only configuration that makes sense."

Hannah was understandably bitter. "I can't believe you're cutting me out of this."

"I promise to make it up to you later." Cooper swooped in and gave her a quick kiss, ignoring the amused glances Tyler and Jackie shared. "You can yell at me later if it will make you feel better."

"It's going to take a lot of effort to make it up to me," Hannah warned.

"I think I'm up to the challenge."

TWELVE

*B*oone met Cooper on the street in front of the Lincoln house. He didn't look happy about the interruption to his morning, but Cooper didn't really care.

"Before you say anything, I have a good reason for calling you here," the security chief offered by way of greeting. He didn't wait for Boone to respond, instead launching into Hannah's terrifying story from the night before. When he finished, Boone was thoughtful.

"Do you really think there was a demon in her apartment?" he asked finally.

Cooper could do nothing but shrug. "I don't know. I'm having trouble with the demon thing, although I'm doing my best to keep that to myself. She doesn't react well when she thinks I'm doubting her."

"What are our other options?"

"Astra. She knows Hannah thinks she's dealing with a demon. It's possible Astra conjured ... whatever it was ... to terrorize Hannah. She's still convinced she'll be able to claim Casper Creek as her own before it's all said and done."

"Does she plan on doing that by running Hannah out of town?"

"That's exactly how."

Boone scowled. "Well, we're not going to let that happen," he said, making up his mind on the spot. "We can handle Astra after the fact. If she's the one doing this, we'll be able to shut her down. It's the boy that concerns me. He's ... weird."

Cooper bit back a chuckle. "He's definitely weird, and not in a fun way. Everyone basically says the same thing when they come into contact with him. He's odd and there's something off about him."

"I don't like casting aspersions on kids — not even my own and she's a righteous pain in the behind — but there's definitely something wrong in this scenario. If the kid isn't a demon, then he's a sociopath. He didn't show one moment of true emotion yesterday. Not one. I was watching him."

Cooper turned rueful. "I was watching him, too. I think we need to test him."

"Test him?"

"Yeah. Jackie gave me some tests we can run to see if we're dealing with a demon."

"And what do those tests entail?"

"Um ... ." Cooper drew his phone out of his pocket and checked the list he'd made before leaving Casper Creek. "We should check the kid's reflection in a mirror. It will look different, like distorted. Jackie described it like those scenes in that old movie *The Ring*."

Boone made a face. "So ... I'm supposed to pick up the kid and shove him in front of a mirror?"

"I think we'll have to be more subtle than that."

"I hope you have other tests."

"I do. Demons react negatively to salt, don't like warm temperatures because it reminds them of being in Hell, know more than they should be able to know, and react poorly to religious symbolism, like crosses and pentagrams."

Boone folded his arms across his chest. "You can't be serious. That's how we're going to test him?"

Cooper nodded. "I have a cross in my back pocket and I figure there will be salt in the house if we need another test."

"I just can't even ... ." Boone shook his head and then straightened his shoulders. "Okay. I'm with you on this. If it gets weird, though, I'm pulling out and you're on your own. The last thing I need is a grieving woman running to the newspapers because I threw salt on her kid and tried to cast the devil out."

Despite the serious situation, Cooper laughed. "Do you ever wonder how we get ourselves into these situations?"

"Every single day of my life."

HANNAH WAS FRUSTRATED. SHE HATED being left behind — this was her theory they were testing, after all — and the fact that Casper Creek was again closed thanks to interference from the state pathologist had her in a tizzy. She could've returned to her apartment and taken a nap, which she desperately needed, but instead she headed for the creek.

She had more ideas, questions she wanted to bounce off someone, and it seemed she'd reached the limit on Jackie's information on the subject. That meant she had to seek out someone else, and the only other person she could think to approach was Astra.

Although the white-haired siren wasn't at the creek when she arrived, Hannah settled down with her back against a tree to wait. She had no doubt the witch would show up eventually ... and she wasn't disappointed.

"I knew you would be back." Astra beamed as she slid into the shade provided by the tree on the other side of the creek.

A magical barrier had been erected to keep her out of Casper Creek and the line ended on that side of the water. The barrier had faltered weeks before thanks to tunnels under the town. The coven witches who previously studied under Abigail worked overtime to close them, however, and so far it seemed to be working.

"Yes, well, you're one of the few people who believes me about the demons," Hannah offered. "You said you were going to do some research. I don't suppose you've held up your end of the bargain, have you?"

Astra's eyes twinkled with mirth. "If I say I'm going to do something, I do it. No matter what you hear about me, I'm a woman of my word."

Hannah couldn't stop herself from needling the woman. "Did you promise to help Abigail? Didn't you join her coven and then break to form your own?"

Astra scowled. "That was an entirely different scenario. I never promised to join Abigail's coven forever. That's something I could never follow through on, so I wouldn't bother pretending I could."

"Fair enough." Hannah shifted to get more comfortable. Weariness invaded her very bones, but this conversation was more important than sleep. "I saw something last night." She launched into her story — the complete story, including Logan's visit and the potential snake attack from the afternoon — before she could take the appropriate time to consider whether it was the right course of action. She went with her gut, which told her Astra had nothing to do with the specter that appeared in her apartment. When she was done, she sat back and waited for Astra to respond.

It took the witch longer than Hannah anticipated to find her voice.

"It moved through the wall?"

That wasn't the part of the story Hannah thought Astra

would be fixated on. "Yeah. Why? Is that weird or something?"

"It's odd." Astra rolled her neck and shifted from one foot to the other, considering. "How much do you know about demons?"

"Not much. Jackie only had a little information to share and I haven't had a chance to read much on the subject because I've been busy with other stuff. The mother of this kid is threatening to sue even though they haven't announced a firm cause of death yet."

"I wouldn't worry about the mother." Astra waved off the statement as if she were nothing more than a pesky fly. "People threaten to sue all the time. Once she sits down with an attorney and realizes how much this is going to cost her, she'll change her mind. Unless they can prove malice on your part — which is impossible — she has no case."

"You sound fairly certain of that."

"I am. The mother isn't going to be a concern for very long. She's grieving. People do crazy things when they're grieving."

That was true. Hannah was hopeful she was right about Lindsey. Right now, however, that wasn't her main concern. "What about the boy?"

"He sounds strange."

Hannah belted out a laugh. "That's the one thing everyone can agree on when it comes to this kid. He's strange ... and he doesn't bother hiding it. If he's not a demon, there's something very weird going on."

"Oh, I'm going to wager he's got a demon inside of him. It would have to be a non-corporeal demon, however. Those are fairly rare these days. Most have been snuffed out."

Hannah was confused. "There's more than one sort of demon?"

Astra bobbed her head. "Think of it like humans. We have

numerous races, mixed races, and so on. It's the same for demons. They're not simply one thing."

"That makes sense. What do you think I should do?"

"You have to exorcise the demon from the boy."

"You say that like it's a normal thing."

"Normal? No. It's doable, however. I can help you ... for a price."

Hannah stilled. She should've seen this coming, she realized. Astra was always going to try and press an advantage. "And what is it you want?"

"I want the grimoire. I know Abigail left it to you. I want it. It should've been mine from the start."

Hannah didn't hesitate before answering. "That's not going to happen."

"Then I want Cooper."

Hannah almost fell over she was so surprised. "Excuse me?"

Astra didn't back down. "You heard me. Cooper was mine long before you came to town. I want him back. He should be mine again. That's not going to happen as long as you're whispering in his ear."

Hannah was flabbergasted. When she finally found her voice, it took everything she had not to fly off the handle. "Cooper is his own person. He's not mine to give."

"You're together. Are you going to sit there and deny it?"

Hannah worked her jaw. "I can't deny it, but we haven't defined what we are together. It's the beginning. He's most certainly not my property, however."

"If you back away from him, he'll come back to me."

"I don't believe that. It doesn't matter, though. I don't want to push Cooper away and there's nothing you could offer me that would cause me to do that. If that's what you want, you're going to be bitterly disappointed. I won't ever trade a person."

Astra blinked several times in rapid succession and then shook her head. "Fine. I don't expect anything in return." She looked disgusted ... in herself. "I just thought I would try. As for the demon, he's dangerous. We must kill him."

"We have to get him out of Logan first." Hannah was firm. "We can't attack the demon as long as the boy is at risk. There has to be a way to get the demon out of there."

"We need to cast him out."

"Do you know how to do that?"

"I think I do. It will require more research, though."

"Then you'd best get on that. I don't think we have a lot of time."

LINDSEY WAS SURPRISED TO FIND Cooper and Boone on her front porch. After warning them that she had every intention of suing Hannah — whether they liked it or not — she allowed the two men into the home. They said they had questions and if they could ultimately provide answers on her husband's death, she was more than willing to entertain them.

"What do you want?" she asked as she sat at her kitchen table and sipped from a mug of coffee. She offered some to the men, but they both politely declined.

"We want to know about your time at Casper Creek," Boone hedged. He'd decided to treat this as he would any other interrogation. Sure, he was trying to get a child alone so he could question him about being a demon, but that didn't mean additional information wouldn't be welcome.

"Why?" Lindsey's face was blank. "I've already told you what happened."

"You have, but we're still trying to nail down the time-line," Cooper offered smoothly. "We don't know that it will be any help, but we have questions ... and it's never good when there are questions of this nature in a death investigation."

Lindsey rolled her eyes. "Fine. Ask away. If I don't like any of the questions, though, I won't be answering them."

"Fair enough." Boone launched into his spiel, giving Cooper a chance to survey the room. Patrick was nowhere to be found — perhaps the boy was out with friends, or at school — but Logan was watching from the open archway that led to the living room. He didn't look happy at the interruption.

After a few minutes, when Cooper was certain Lindsey was rapt up with whatever Boone was talking about, he slowly slid away from the table and approached the boy.

"How's it going?" he asked in his most amiable voice.

The boy looked at him with dead eyes. "My father is dead."

"I know. I'm sorry to hear that. You must miss him a great deal."

"Not really. He yelled all the time." Obviously bored, Logan surveyed his fingernails for a moment and then looked past Cooper so he could focus on his mother. "She's not much better, though."

Cooper didn't trust the kid, but he couldn't hide his surprise at the callous way he spoke about his parents. "There must be something good about her."

"Nope."

"I'm sure she tucked you in and read you stories when you were a little kid."

"She's too lazy to do that."

Lindsey pushed away from the table and got to her feet, drawing Cooper's attention. "I think I have some medical records in the office," she explained to Boone. She hadn't paid a wisp of attention to Cooper and her youngest child. "I can let you look at the records."

"I would appreciate that," Boone said, remaining in his chair.

Lindsey flashed a tight smile in Cooper's direction before skirting around her son. The second she was gone, Cooper decided to take advantage of the situation. He angled himself so he could see into the mirror on the wall. It was an antique, silver frame, and he was eager to see Logan's reflection in it. Unfortunately for him, Logan was standing just outside the arc where he could be seen.

"Come here," Cooper instructed, gesturing for the boy to move closer.

"I'm good here," Logan replied.

Cooper clenched his jaw. "Just ... come here."

"No thanks."

Cooper looked to Boone for help, but the sheriff was busy filling his hand with salt from the shaker on the table. Logan's eyes narrowed to dangerous slits when he saw what Boone was doing.

"You shouldn't make a mess," he intoned, shifting from one foot to the other. He looked ready to bolt should Boone try tossing the salt in his direction.

If Cooper wasn't suspicious before, the boy's understanding of what was about to happen would've tipped him over the edge. He decided to play things a different way. "We know what you are," he said finally, keeping an ear open for Lindsey's return. He would rather the woman not hear him accusing her son of being a demon. "We know what you're doing."

"Do you?" Logan's eyes lit with mirth as he snickered. His response made him seem older. "What is it you think I'm doing?"

"You're a demon," Cooper replied, not missing a beat. "Don't bother denying it."

Boone made a groaning noise. "I can't believe you just said that."

Cooper ignored his reaction. "I want you to stay away from Hannah," he warned. "Don't even think about going near her again."

Logan's smile only widened. "Are you threatening me?"

"Don't think of it as a threat. Think of it as a promise."

"Well, in that case ... ." He sauntered into the room, taking up a position directly in front of the mirror. There, in the reflection, Cooper saw the confirmation he'd been looking for. The boy's features were twisted to the point where he looked as if he had horns growing out of his head.

"Holy ... ." Boone's mouth dropped open as he stared into the mirror. It was obvious, right up until this moment, he had his doubts about what they would find. Those doubts disappeared with his shaky gasp.

"I have no interest in your witch," Logan supplied, his eyes flashing with malice. "I find her interesting, don't get me wrong, but she doesn't have enough power to tempt me. How about we make a deal?"

Cooper swallowed hard. His mouth had gone dry. It was one thing to suspect, even lob accusations, but to have the proof standing directly in front of him was jarring. "What sort of deal?"

"I'll leave the witch alone if you go away and never come back."

"We can't make that promise," Boone replied, shaking his head. "We're going to get you out of that boy whether you like it or not."

The laugh Logan let loose was something straight out of a horror movie. It would've made more sense coming from a demented clown rather than a ten-year-old. "You're so funny ... and weak. You don't have the power to take me on. Neither does that witch you seem so intent on protecting. I wonder what her insides would look like spread across the floor."

Cooper's temper flared. "You're going to stay away from her," he hissed, hunkering down so he was at eye level with the child. "Don't go near her. Stay away from Casper Creek."

"I do what I want ... when I want. You can't stop me."

"I wouldn't be so sure of that."

The boy — er, demon — blinked several times and then adopted a lazy smile. "I think we're going to have a lot of fun playing together. How about you?"

Cooper wasn't sure how to respond. "Stay away from Hannah."

"Oh, it's too late for that. You should've agreed to stay away. Now I'm not going to have a choice but to fight you."

"You'll lose."

"You'd like to think that, wouldn't you? I've been around longer than you've been alive. I'll still be kicking it when you're long gone. There's not a thing you can do about it."

He sounded sure of himself, but Cooper was determined. No matter what, he would protect Hannah ... and get that creature out of the boy. Nothing could stop him now. He wouldn't rest until Logan was free and Hannah had her life back.

There was no turning back now.

THIRTEEN

"*W*e have to get the demon out."

Hannah was matter-of-fact as she sat at one of the saloon tables, her hands resting on top of the wooden surface, her fingers constantly clenching and unclenching.

Cooper had been eager to get back to her, the boy's demeanor setting his teeth on edge. He was an antsy mess until they were reunited. Even then he couldn't refrain from pulling her in for a long hug, which seemed to amuse Tyler and the other coven members Jackie had called for backup.

"We need to think long and hard about what we're going to do," Cooper corrected, leaning back in his chair. Now that he was away from Logan, he was feeling braver. He would never forget the chilling look on the boy's face, though. It would haunt him for aas long as he lived.

"What's to think about?" Hannah challenged. "He's a little boy. He's being ... invaded. We have to help him."

"I agree we need to think about helping him."

She shook her head, firm. "Not think about it. We actually

have to do it. I can't live with the idea that he's trapped in his own head and can't get out."

Cooper frowned. "Where did you come up with that idea?"

Hannah shifted on her chair, suddenly uncomfortable. "Oh, well ... ."

Suspicious, Cooper narrowed his eyes. "You didn't spend your afternoon down by the creek again, did you?"

Instead of lying, or making excuses, Hannah merely shrugged. She was done kowtowing to others. That included Cooper. Sure, he hadn't made demands of her time like previous men in her life had, but she wasn't about to make herself small so someone else could feel large and in charge.

"Astra has information that can help us. I talked to her. It was fine."

Cooper made a strangled sound in the back of his throat. "It was fine?" He was incredulous. "Have you forgotten that one of her acolytes tried to kill you two weeks ago?"

"She didn't have anything to do with that."

"She still terrorized you. She wants what's yours."

Hannah had to swallow her amusement. Cooper had no idea exactly how right he was. However, there was no way she could tell him the whole truth about their conversation in front of an audience, so she held it together. "I'm not pretending Astra is an altruistic soul. She can help us, though. She's researching ways to exorcise the demon."

"I've already been doing that," Jackie volunteered. "I'm pretty sure I can handle it."

Hannah perked up. "Really? Could you handle it today?"

The question clearly caught Jackie off guard. "I don't know. Do you want to do it today?"

"Today is a bad idea," the youngest member of the coven announced, speaking for the first time. Becky Gibbons was twenty-three, blond, and completely enamored with Cooper.

She couldn't stop staring at him even as the others in the saloon discussed freeing a small child from terrible torment. "Cooper is right. We should do whatever he says."

Cooper sent Becky a thankful smile as Jackie and Tyler groaned in unison.

"Cooper is not right," Tyler countered. "We're talking about a little boy here. We have no idea what sort of torture he's enduring. That's on top of the fact that his father is dead. We need to get him out of there."

Boone stirred. He'd been largely silent since returning, but it was obvious he had a lot on his mind. "We're working under the assumption that the demon is what killed Todd Lincoln, right?"

Hannah nodded without hesitation. "Most definitely. How else would he have died?"

"I don't know. The state pathologist refuses to answer that question."

"I'm guessing that's because he doesn't know," Danielle Garrett, the calmest member of the coven, volunteered. "The fact that they can't find a cause of death has to be troublesome to them. They'll wait until they get the toxicology results back before making a firm decision ... and that could take weeks."

Hannah's stomach did a slow, uncomfortable roll. "Does that mean I'll be living in uncertainty until then?"

Sympathy washing over him, Boone patted her hand. "Honey, I know you don't want to hear this, but Lindsey could file a lawsuit years from now. It's not something that is going to magically disappear."

"I know but ... ." Hannah trailed off. She knew better than believing truth would always prevail. She'd worked at a law office for years, for crying out loud. If anyone recognized that justice wasn't blind, it was her. "We have to focus on the most important thing. That's Logan. We need to exorcise the demon. Jackie says she can do it."

"We can all do it together," Jackie corrected. "It's going to take the full coven." Her eyes were heavy when they landed on Hannah. "That's including you."

Hannah visibly gulped, surprised. "Me?" Her eyebrows hopped up her forehead. "You want me to participate?"

"Yeah. It's going to take all of us."

"That's not even our biggest concern," Boone groused. "There's no way Lindsey is simply going to allow us to waltz into the house and perform an exorcism."

Hannah sighed. He was right. "Then we need to get her out of the house."

"Do you have a suggestion on how to do that?"

"Just one."

COOPER WAS STILL RETICENT WHEN the motley group of individuals returned to the Lincoln family's quiet neighborhood. He sat behind the wheel of his truck and pouted as Hannah prepared to hop out and join the others.

"You should probably stay here," she said finally, losing the battle against her temper. "We won't be long. We'll have some food after we save Logan."

Cooper slid her a sidelong look. "I know you think I'm being difficult."

"I think you're trying to protect me, and while sweet, that's not what I want."

"What do you want?" he asked softly.

"I want someone who trusts me."

"And you don't think I do?"

"I think you believe you need to take care of me. I lived with someone who thought the same thing for a long time. He also happened to think I was an idiot, which led to a different set of problems, but at the heart of it he thought I couldn't function without him. I don't want someone who thinks like that."

He was thoughtful as he ran his hand over her hair. "You still haven't answered the question. What do you want?"

"A partner, not a boss."

He sighed, the sound long and drawn out. "I'm not trying to boss you around."

"I know. You're trying to protect me, which is a noble thing. That's still not what I want. We need to work together. If we're not equals, this is never going to work."

He stilled. "You believe I don't think we're equals."

"I believe you're a good man who likes to be in charge," she clarified. "I get it. I need to be seen as an equal, though. And, while I know I'm new to this and haven't yet figured everything out, I want to try. You have to give me that."

He held her gaze for a long beat and then wordlessly nodded.

"Does that mean you're going to work with me here?"

"Yes." He answered without hesitation, killing the engine of the truck and pocketing the keys. "Boone managed to call in a favor with the funeral home. Lindsey is on her way to talk to the funeral director. That means the boys are alone inside."

Hannah flashed a smile. It was small but heartfelt. "Thank you."

He squeezed her hand, stopping her before she could climb out of the truck. "I'm going to do my absolute best," he promised. "There are going to be times when my baser urges take over, though. If I feel you're in danger, I'm not going to be able to stop myself from trying to protect you."

"I think that's a natural instinct. You can't always shut me down, though."

"That's not what I was trying to do."

"I know." She felt markedly better when she reached over the console to hug him. "We're going to figure this out."

"We are," he agreed, snagging her chin between his fingers and holding her in place so he could give her a quick kiss. "Let's do this, huh?"

She beamed at him. "See. This won't be so bad."

Cooper was slower than her getting out of the truck, the rest of their group already gathered on the sidewalk. He didn't miss the way Becky glared at him when he moved to the spot at Hannah's side.

"Boone is parked on the highway," he announced. "He'll be watching in case Lindsey turns around. The funeral home has promised to keep her there for at least an hour — although we're aiming for two — so we have to move fast."

Jackie clutched a bag of supplies next to her chest and nodded. She looked nervous, which didn't exactly make Hannah feel better. She opened her mouth to suggest they get moving when a scream ripped from inside the house and caught everybody's attention.

"What was that?" Tyler asked, taking a step toward the house and staring at the second floor.

"Patrick," Hannah answered without hesitation. "He's in trouble. Logan is going after him. We have to get to him."

Cooper didn't even try to stop her when she started jogging across the road. She was determined. So was he. The idea of her suffering from low self-esteem despite how great she was bothered him. He blamed this ex-boyfriend, making a mental note to visit him one day so they could have a serious talk, but applauded Hannah for wanting to make herself a better person, a stronger woman. This was the first step, and he intended to be with her when she embarked on her new journey.

By silent agreement, they headed for the back door. People on the street might ask questions if they witnessed them going through the front ... and they were questions nobody wanted to answer. Cooper slid ahead of Hannah when they reached their destination and he ignored the dirty look she shot him when he reached for the door.

"I'm head of security," he reminded her. "That means I go through the door first."

"I didn't agree to that."

"Well, you're going to have to get over it. If I'm supposed to treat you like a partner, respect your position, you need to do the same for me. As head of security, I'm in charge when we go on outings like this."

Hannah narrowed her eyes. "Do you think we'll go on a lot of outings like this?"

"Probably more than either of us will be comfortable with. We're going to have to suck it up and learn to compromise."

"I can do that."

He grinned as he popped open the door. "Me, too." He slid in ahead of her as Becky made a series of grumbling noises. It was obvious what she was complaining about, but no one had the time or energy to put up with her.

"Where?" Tyler asked as he joined the small club in the kitchen.

Cooper shook his head. "I don't ... ." He didn't get a chance to finish because, from the second floor, another scream careened through the house. "Stay behind me," he ordered when Hannah raced toward the stairs.

The group pounded up the narrow steps, Cooper and Hannah arriving on the scene first. There, they found the oddest of scenes.

Logan stood outside a closed door, his eyes flashing red as he beat against the wood and kicked at the trim. "Let me in!" he screeched, completely ignoring the new guests.

"Go away, Logan." Patrick sounded petrified on the other

side of the door. Hannah could hear moving furniture, as if he was trying to barricade himself in his bedroom. "Just leave me alone."

"Oh, it's far too late for that," Logan intoned. "You shouldn't have said what you did."

"I didn't mean it!"

"You meant it, and I can't let you repeat it. You'll tell the wrong people and ruin things for me. I can't let that happen. You shouldn't have been eavesdropping when that rent-a-cop and the sheriff were visiting earlier. I didn't even think you were here. You should've kept your mouth shut."

"I was just asking a question!" Patrick started sobbing on the other side of the door as Logan redoubled his efforts. "Just ... leave me alone. I'm sorry. I'm sorry. I'm ... ." His words became garbled.

"We have to stop this," Hannah announced, her eyes flashing. "We can't let this go on."

Slowly, Logan stopped kicking the door and tracked his eyes to Hannah. He seemed surprised by the home invasion ... although he didn't look nervous in the least. "What are you doing here?"

"We were just about to ask you the same thing," Cooper replied. He wasn't equipped with a weapon, but he stretched out an arm to keep Hannah back as he faced off with the boy. "I told you I would be back."

"Yes, but I had no idea it would be today. You really are an idiot, aren't you?" Logan snorted at his own joke before focusing on Hannah. "At least you brought me something pretty to play with."

"You're not going to touch her," Cooper hissed. "I told you that earlier. If you touch her, I'll ... ."

"What?" Logan challenged. "What is it that you're going to do to me? You don't have the power to stop me. She doesn't either. She might be interesting, a plaything of sorts, but she's not capable of taking me out."

"She's not alone," Jackie announced, moving into the space behind Cooper and joining hands with Danielle and Becky. "We'll all be doing this together."

"Oh, really?" Logan remained calm. "And what is it you think you'll be doing?"

"I guess you'll just have to wait and see." Jackie gestured for Hannah to join them. "We need four corners," she instructed. "You have to participate."

Hannah cast one lingering look in Cooper's direction, but he inclined his head to get her to move.

"I'll be okay," he promised. "Do what you have to do."

On impulse, Hannah pressed a firm kiss to his lips and then moved to the spot between Danielle and Jackie. She linked her hands with theirs without hesitation, and then lifted her head to the sky as the other witches began to chant.

"How sweet," Logan called out, mirth practically rolling off him in waves. "I can't wait to get my hands on that sweetness. I'm going to rip her apart from the inside and treat her as yummy appetizer for my next act."

Cooper openly glared at the creature. He could no longer think of it as a little boy. "I'll never let you touch her."

"You don't have the strength to stop me." Logan took a menacing step in Cooper's direction at the same moment the witches started chanting even louder, the sound more powerful.

Hannah had no idea how she was following the spell. It was in Latin, a language she didn't know, and yet the words somehow seemed to come naturally. Once Jackie started repeating the same phrases over and over again, Hannah joined in without any prodding. There were four voices whispering throughout the second floor of the house, but they sounded like one.

"Stop that!" For the first time since realizing he had company, Logan looked legitimately worried. "Stop that right now!" His voice was unnaturally high.

"Oh, now you're afraid," Cooper taunted, his eyes slanting. "You realize that you're about to fall and you're afraid. Maybe you're getting a small sampling of the fear you put into Logan, huh?"

The creature snorted, his eyes wild. "Oh, you have no idea what you're even talking about." His head swung from left to right and then he tried to bolt around Cooper in a desperate attempt to make it down the stairs. "Let me go!"

Cooper grabbed him around the waist, holding tight. "I can't let that happen." Even though Logan was small, he put up a terrific fight. "Tyler, I need your help," Cooper grunted as the boy landed a hard elbow in his stomach.

Tyler didn't think twice; he threw himself into the melee. He was on his knees, helping Cooper hold the child in place, as the spell grew. Flashes of magic began bouncing off the walls and the terror emanating from Logan was palpable.

"No! You're killing me! Patrick, help me!"

Realizing what the creature was trying to do — create a distraction — Cooper held firm. "Patrick, stay in that room. This will all be over in a second. It will be better after that."

Patrick merely continued to sob on the other side of the door.

Hannah, completely lost to the spell, started funneling more magic into the ritual. She felt drained and yet exhilarated ... and then the wall of magic stood up straight before barreling toward the boy.

"No!" Logan viciously fought against Tyler and Cooper, but it was already too late. The magic rushed into him, immediately knocking the boy to the ground.

Cooper and Tyler scrambled away from the magic out of instinct, but it remained in the center of the room, bursting through Logan's body like a nuclear explosion ... although keeping him whole the entire time. The magic built to a crescendo, thunder echoing through the house, and then it was over as quickly as it had started and Logan remained prone on the floor.

"Well, that was interesting," Tyler muttered, dragging a hand through his hair.

"I'll say." Cooper shifted to check on Logan, letting out a relieved sigh when he realized the boy was still alive. "I really hope that worked because it's too much for my heart to take if we have to do it again."

Tyler laughed ... and then coughed ... and then went wide-eyed when he heard footsteps on top of the stairs.

As if tied together, everyone from the Casper Creek contingent turned in that direction in unison ... only to find Lindsey staring at them with incredulous eyes.

"Just what the hell is going on here?"

Hannah thought she might fall over. "Uh-oh."

All Cooper could do was shake his head. Uh-oh was right.

FOURTEEN

*L*indsey's fury was palpable. Her confusion was almost overwhelming. Panic gripped Hannah by the throat and didn't let go. Cooper was the first to speak.

"This isn't what you think," he offered.

Lindsey glared at him and moved toward Logan, who was just beginning to stir on the floor. "Oh, really? And what is it I'm supposed to think?"

"Well ... ."

"Tell her we're selling Girl Scout cookies," Becky suggested on a whisper.

Tyler shot her a disdainful look. "Yeah. That should fly."

Hannah swallowed hard and searched for an explanation that would make sense. It wasn't surprising that she came up with nothing. "Um ... ."

Patrick picked that moment to open the door. His dark hair was disheveled and he looked perplexed. First, his gaze dropped to his brother. Then, slowly, he tracked all the faces in the room. He didn't speak.

"What is going on here?" Lindsey practically shrieked. "I'm being serious. I want an explanation right now!"

"We were checking on the boys," Cooper offered lamely. "We had a bad feeling they were in trouble and ... well ... we just wanted to make sure they were okay."

"You wanted to make sure my sons were okay?" Lindsey was incredulous. "I can't even ... I'm calling the police." She dug in her pocket for her phone as Hannah looked to Cooper for help.

Patrick was the one who finally spoke up. "They saved me, Mom." His voice was low but firm. "They only ran in because they heard me yelling."

That wasn't entirely true, but Cooper enthusiastically bobbed his head. "Yes. We heard Patrick screaming and came running."

Patrick made a face. "I wasn't screaming. Guys don't scream. I was yelling kinda loud, though."

Cooper wasn't in a position to argue, so he didn't. "Fair enough. You were yelling ... loudly."

"Why were you yelling?" Lindsey's face was bare of makeup and she looked haggard, as if she hadn't been sleeping. Hannah figured that was probably the case since the woman was essentially navigating her way through a living nightmare.

"Because Logan was being ... ." Patrick searched for the right words.

Cooper took pity on him and cleared his throat. "Ma'am, I think it's possible that your son is disturbed." He gripped his hands together and barreled forward. "He's been showing signs of aggressive behavior."

"I'll say," Hannah muttered under her breath.

"Aggressive behavior?" Lindsey looked to be working herself up into another lather. "He's ten. What sort of aggressive behavior could he be displaying?"

"He tried to kill me," Patrick replied in a sullen voice. "He was going after me, trying to kick in the door of my bedroom, and kept threatening he was going to rip my throat out."

Lindsey blinked her eyes several times in rapid succession. Finally, she shook her head. "No. He's a good boy."

"He's a monster," Patrick countered.

"He's just acting out because of what happened to your father," Lindsey argued. "He's upset."

"He's been a monster since before then," Patrick argued. "Besides ... I think he might've been the one to kill Dad."

Lindsey's mouth dropped open as shocked horror washed over her features. "How could you say that?"

"He disappeared right before we were supposed to get on the chairlift," Patrick protested. "We were looking for him. You told him to stick close and he disappeared. Dad was supposed to be right behind us, but he never made it.

"Logan was angry at him before that," he continued. "Dad kept yelling at us — he was always yelling at us — and Logan didn't like it. He said right before he disappeared that we would be better without Dad."

"You take that back!" Lindsey jabbed a finger in her oldest son's direction, fury evident. "Your father was a good man."

"Not really." Patrick was morose. "He yelled all the time. He blamed Logan for everything that happened in the house. Have you forgotten that? He blamed him for the headaches."

Lindsey shook her head. "Stop talking," she hissed. Hannah noted she'd yet to kneel next to her son, check on him. Logan remained on the floor. He looked to be dazed and confused and yet his mother never as much as looked at him.

"You're just saying all this because these people got to you," she continued. "They came here to convince you to talk to me, get me to drop the lawsuit. Admit it."

"I haven't talked to them, Mom," Patrick argued. "I didn't even see them until I opened the door. I could hear them trying to talk to Logan, but he didn't care. He kept threatening them, said he was going to kill her." He gestured toward Hannah. "There's something wrong with him. How can you not see that?"

"There's nothing wrong with him." Lindsey was practically growling now. "He's just a boy who is ... grieving."

"Then why won't you look at him?" Hannah asked finally. She couldn't ignore what she was seeing. "You've avoided eye contact with him since you got here. You haven't even asked him if he's okay."

"He's obviously okay," Lindsey shot back. "I mean ... look at him." She finally forced her gaze to the boy on the floor. "No thanks to you, of course. I'll take him to the doctor after the police come to arrest these ... cretins."

"They saved me, Mom," Patrick repeated, firmer this time. "If the police question me, that's exactly what I'm going to tell them."

"And I'll explain how these people have brainwashed you. I'm not listening to another second of this." She pulled out her phone and stared at the screen. She seemed to be momentarily lost.

The sound of pounding feet on the stairs was enough to draw her attention. It was Boone joining the party ... and he wasn't alone. He had several police officers with him, and they were all dressed in uniforms.

"What's going on?" Cooper asked, confused.

"Yeah, what's going on?" Tyler intoned. "A heads-up that we were about to be invaded might've been nice."

Boone pretended he didn't hear him and focused his full attention on Cooper. "I got a call on the road. The locals wanted to inform me that they'd come to a conclusion on Todd Lincoln."

Hannah's stomach clenched. "What did they find?"

"They haven't technically found anything yet, but they're

testing for poison," Boone replied, his expression unreadable. "The thing is ... you're no longer a suspect, Hannah. You never really were. The state pathologist, in conjunction with the Cedar Spring Police Department, were always looking at a different suspect."

Lindsey shook her head at the news. "No. She's to blame." She jutted her chin in Hannah's direction. "She killed my husband. Sure, maybe she didn't do it with her own hands, but she's definitely to blame. It was either her or her people."

"It wasn't." Boone was firm. "Ma'am, why didn't you tell us about Eleanor Rich?"

Lindsey furrowed her brow, confused. "Eleanor? You mean the old woman who lived on the corner?"

Boone bobbed his head. "She was your neighbor for ten years ... and she's dead."

"What does that have to do with me?"

"Technically, it doesn't have anything to do with you." Boone moved to the side as the officers piled into the small space. It was only then that Hannah realized their attention was fixated on Logan. They weren't looking at anyone else.

"I don't understand," Lindsey argued. "What is going on?"

"This is Detective Shoemaker," Boone replied. "He has some things to discuss with you." Boone calmly drew Hannah away from Cooper and Logan and secured her along the wall with him. His gaze never left the boy.

"I'm Aaron Shoemaker," the detective introduced himself with grim resolve. "We've met once before, ma'am. Do you remember?"

Lindsey was clearly bewildered. "I think I remember. You were asking questions right after Eleanor's body was found. I assumed that was because she was in the house so long without anyone realizing she'd passed."

"It's more than that, ma'am." Shoemaker was the picture of professionalism. "There's no easy way to put this so I'm just going to lay it out for you. For the past three months, we've been investigating Ms. Rich's death. We expected to find that she'd died of natural causes. That was not, however, the case.

"After an extensive medical investigation, we found that she was poisoned," he continued. "It was a homemade concoction, complete with hemlock and some other herbs that when mixed together, caused death. The thing is, the poison had to be administered over the course of several days. Do you know why that's important?"

Lindsey blankly shook her head. "Should I?"

"When we talked to neighbors, they said your son was often seen at her house," Shoemaker continued. "They said he was a frequent visitor."

"So what?" Lindsey's temper was back on display. "He volunteered his time to help her. He's a good boy. That's what he does."

"No one else in the neighborhood seems to think he's a good boy," Shoemaker countered. "Your neighbors across the street, the Fredricks, believe he killed their cat."

"Oh, that's preposterous. Their cat ran away."

"And the dog one block over? Did he run away, too?"

"How should I know? It's not my dog."

Shoemaker looked as if he was at the end of his rope. "Ma'am, the one thing everyone in this neighborhood could agree on is that your son is odd. They say he's mean to the other kids, bullies them, and kids three times his size are terrified of him."

"That is nonsense." Even as she said the words, Lindsey's expression changed. It was as if she was thinking ... and thinking hard. "My son is not capable of what you're accusing him of."

"We don't happen to believe that's true. He'll have the opportunity to defend himself in court, however."

"Court?" Lindsey's eyes went wide. "You can't be serious."

"I'm serious."

"And what are you charging him with, killing a dog and a cat?"

"No, he's being charged with first-degree murder for Eleanor Rich's death."

"But ... no."

"I'm sorry." Shoemaker withdrew a set of cuffs from his belt and focused on the child. "Logan Lincoln, you're under arrest. You have the right to remain silent. Anything you say can and will be used against you in a court of law. Do you understand your rights as they've been explained to you?"

And just like that, things got worse. Hannah wasn't even sure that was possible.

AFTER ANSWERING A SERIES OF QUESTIONS about what they were doing inside the Lincoln house — and with some serious backup on Boone's account — the Casper Creek group was released and admonished to stay away from the family. The coven members opted to stop for dinner on their way home, which left Tyler, Cooper, and Hannah when it was time to head back.

Hannah opted to sit in the backseat, her mind busy. She couldn't believe what had transpired.

"Do you want to order pizza or something?" Cooper asked when he parked at the saloon.

It took a few minutes for the words to penetrate the haze invading Hannah's mind. "What?" She looked confused when she finally focused on Cooper's face.

"Dinner," he prodded. "You should really have something to eat."

"I'm not hungry." In fact, she felt sick to her stomach. "I don't think I'll ever be able to eat again after this."

"Oh, good. Drama." Cooper forced a wan smile. "I think that's exactly what we need to make this night complete."

She managed to muster a scowl. "I'm not being dramatic. This is ... unbelievable. They took that little boy to prison."

"It sounds like he had it coming," Tyler noted as Cooper helped Hannah down from the truck. "I mean ... who kills a dog? He deserves to rot in prison for the rest of his life."

"Yes, because the dog's death is more troublesome than the old woman he poisoned," Cooper drawled.

"At least she had a good life," Tyler objected.

"Let's just agree that they're both traumatic deaths and leave it at that," Cooper suggested,. "I just can't believe the cops have been looking at that kid for months. If they'd moved faster, his father would still be alive."

"You guys are missing the point," Hannah said finally, finding her voice. "The boy didn't do any of those things. It was the demon inside of him that did. Now he's free of the demon, but he's going to be locked up forever for things he didn't do."

"That's a fair point," Tyler muttered.

"You can't worry about that," Cooper insisted, reaching for her so they could share a hug. "We did what we could for him. He's free. Besides ... he's a kid. At ten, there's no way they'll manage to lock him up forever. It's far more likely he'll go to a home until he's twenty-one and then be released back into society."

Hannah frowned. "That doesn't make me feel better."

"Me either but there's literally nothing we can do about it. What are we supposed to do? We can't go in front of a judge and tell him it was a demon. We'll get laughed out of court ... or perhaps locked up ourselves. We can't intervene."

"Boone knows the truth," Tyler added. "Maybe there's something he can do. He is the sheriff, after all."

Hannah wasn't nearly as placated by the thought as the

two men. "I guess." She rubbed her forehead, weariness taking over. "I'm exhausted."

"You didn't sleep," Cooper reminded her. "You had a busy day on top of everything else, a lot of emotions to deal with. We should go to bed."

The unintended slip made Hannah smile. "*We?*"

"Oh, snap." Tyler made a hilarious face as he danced around.

Cooper glared at him and then held up his hand to symbolically shut Tyler out of the conversation. "I just meant that we're both tired. You need rest ... and I need rest ... and we should probably do it separately."

Hannah pursed her lips in amusement. "That's probably a very good idea. Sleep, I mean. Separately."

"Shot down again," Tyler intoned.

Cooper made a hysterical face. "How about I walk with you to collect Jinx at Arnie's place? Then I'll make sure you're tucked in tight for the night. I'll even come back tomorrow morning with a big breakfast. I'm sure you'll be hungry then."

Something occurred to Hannah. "Will the park open again tomorrow?"

"It should. I'll handle calling the employees."

"*I'll* handle calling the employees," Tyler corrected. "You two need sleep ... and to prepare for what I assume will be an adorable breakfast date. I suggest Hannah wear blue because it will bring out her eyes and Coop can practice flexing in the mirror tonight so he looks extra good."

Cooper flicked his friend's ear. "You are, without a doubt, the biggest pain in the behind. I just can't deal with you."

The interaction was enough to pull a legitimate smile from Hannah. "Oh, you guys are so cute. Have you ever considered that you're the couple to watch at Casper Creek?"

Cooper snickered. "It's been mentioned a time or two." He put his hand to the small of her back and prodded her toward Main Street. "Come on. We'll collect Jinx and get you settled. I think a good ten hours of sleep is exactly what the doctor ordered."

Hannah offered Tyler a half-wave and then fell into step with Cooper. She wasn't quite ready to let her woe go. "I know you don't want to hear it, but we really need to think of a way to help Logan. It's not his fault he was possessed."

"No," Cooper agreed. "It's not his fault. I don't see how we have a say in the matter, though. This is beyond our scope."

"Do you think it's beyond Boone's scope?"

"Probably not, but we need to be smart about it. There's nothing we can do tonight. That includes Boone. We'll do our best to talk to him tomorrow. That's all we can do."

It wasn't much, but it was something. Hannah reluctantly bobbed her head. "I really am exhausted. I had no idea it was possible to be this tired."

"Are you sure you're okay staying alone?" The look on her face was enough to have him scrambling. "I just mean that I could stay with you if you're feeling uneasy over what happened last night. I would stay on the couch or something."

Hannah laughed at his discomfort, delighted. "Oh, you really are cute." She planted a warm kiss on his cheek. "As for the offer, I appreciate it. The demon is gone, though. We exorcised it."

"From the boy. I don't necessarily know that you killed the demon. He could still be alive ... just without a body for the time being."

Hannah hadn't considered that. Ultimately, she shook her head. "No, I'll be fine. Even if the demon managed to escape, he's weak. He won't come back here. He'll run."

Cooper could only hope she was right.

FIFTEEN

*H*annah found herself on edge when it came time to wind down. Even though she had Jinx at her side — and he seemed perfectly normal — she couldn't stop herself from turning on every light the entire apartment. She didn't want to leave any shadows behind for the demon to hide in should he return.

She'd spoken the truth to Cooper. She was convinced that the demon had either fled or was so seriously hurt he couldn't possibly regroup this fast. That didn't soothe her frazzled nerves, though. She was jumpy.

In an effort to relax, she filled the tub with steaming water and dropped in a relaxing bath bomb before sinking into the water to her chin and closing her eyes. The exhaustion overwhelming her was profound, matching by the sadness she felt when thinking about Logan.

Life wasn't fair. She told herself that daily. Other people told her that, too. If anyone should know about the unfair nature of life, it was her. She'd done everything she could to make a man happy, only to have it blow up in her face.

She lost her job, the future she envisioned, and her pride.

On top of that, she found she had a grandmother she was unfairly kept away from who was desperate to get to know her and had secrets to share. None of that could be fixed. She could only move forward and not look back.

Still, it bothered her. Thinking of Logan being punished for things he hadn't done, that some creature from another world had perpetuated while wearing his face, was another crushing blow.

Even though her mind was busy, Hannah managed to eventually shut down. She was floating on fatigue and regret when the water cooled to the point she could no longer tolerate it. She let loose a heavy sigh before exiting the tub, wrapping herself in the robe she kept hanging on the back of the bathroom door.

She paused in the hallway long enough to look into her bedroom. Jinx was already spread out on the center of the bed, his head on a pillow. She would have to move him to make enough room for herself. Still, the sight of him snoring away made her happy.

She was safe, she reminded herself. Nothing was going to happen. The odds were astronomical against the demon returning.

She believed that right up until the point she strolled into the living room, determined to shut off the lights, and came face to face with a shadow.

"Oh, my ... ." She veered hard to her right to avoid the creature, careening into the hallway wall as she fought to keep her footing. She was stunned, her heart pounding so hard she thought she might pass out, and her voice was nothing but a whiny screech.

"You," the demon hissed. "This is your doing."

Hannah's eyelids fluttered, but she managed to keep from passing out through sheer force of will. If she lost consciousness now, she would die. She was certain of that. Whatever

157

this thing was — a remnant of a more powerful creature, the black soul of the demon who turned Logan into a murderer, something else entirely — it could still kill her. It looked weak, drained, but there was death in its murderous red eyes.

"What are you?" she asked when she finally managed to control her breathing enough to speak. Her voice cracked as she leaned against the wall, keeping as much distance between her and the creature as possible.

"Shouldn't you have asked that question before you performed your little ritual?"

"You were possessing that boy. You made him do things ... horrible things."

"You don't even know what you're talking about," the creature raged, blowing out enough power to send a vase spinning across the room. It smacked into the wall behind the couch and shattered into a million pieces.

The noise was enough to rouse Jinx in the other room and the dog rushed out, his jaws snapping. Hannah, on instinct, wrapped her arms around his neck before he could attack the creature. The thought of the demon doing anything to hurt her beloved canine companion was more than she could take.

"Don't hurt him," she yelled as she used all of her body weight to keep Jinx in the hallway. "You just surprised him. He won't hurt you."

The demon was incredulous. "He looks as if he wants to eat me for dinner."

"Don't hurt him!"

The demon, who looked more solid than ethereal, remained rooted to his spot, clearly undecided. Then the unmistakable sound of pounding steps on the stairs that led to the apartment filled the room.

Help was near, Hannah realized. Someone had heard her scream, realized she was in trouble, and was coming to the rescue. She hated herself for wanting to be saved but she was so out of her element she didn't know what to do.

Banging started on the door almost immediately.

"Hannah! Are you okay?"

It was Tyler. Hannah's eyes jerked to the door as she tried to estimate if she could make it across the room and let the veterinarian in without crossing paths with the demon. When she looked back, the creature was gone. He had disappeared again, dissolving into the night.

She was okay.

She was alive.

She was also rigid with fear.

TYLER CALLED COOPER AS SOON as Hannah found the courage to let him into the apartment. Then the animal handler sat with her until Cooper arrived. The security guru was a big ball of nerves when he stormed through the open door, immediately setting his sights on Hannah and rushing to her.

"What happened?" The question was directed to Tyler as he crushed Hannah against his chest.

"The demon was back," Tyler replied, calm. He'd already had his freakout when Hannah explained what she found when exiting the bathroom.

"You saw it?"

Tyler shook his head. "I saw ... something. I don't know how to explain it. Hannah had every light in the place on — I figured she might leave them on the entire night or something — and I wasn't paying all that much attention. Then I heard her yell from downstairs when I was pouring myself a drink. I rushed up right away ... and I heard another voice inside ... but it was gone by the time she let me in."

"Geez." Cooper rubbed his hands over her shaking shoulders. She'd obviously been through the wringer. "How did it get up here?"

"I have no idea. I didn't see anything on the street ... and I was paying attention just to be on the safe side. I'm not sure how it got up here or out."

"Well ... great." Cooper stroked Hannah's hair before leading her to the couch so they could sit. She looked shaken, as if she was barely holding up. He couldn't blame her. She'd gone through more in a few days than most people could tolerate over an entire lifetime. "Look at me, darling," he instructed with a gentle tone. When her blue eyes lifted and he saw the fear reflected there, fury took over. "I'm so sorry. I knew I shouldn't have left."

"I told you to leave," she reminded him, speaking finally. She sounded stronger than she felt, which she was grateful for. "This isn't your fault."

"It's nobody's fault," Tyler countered. "It's something we're going to have to deal with, though. If that thing is still hanging around ... we're going to have to find another way to kill it."

"We'll put Jackie and the others on that first thing in the morning." Cooper swayed back and forth as he continuously rubbed his hands over Hannah's back. "Did it say anything to you, Hannah? Do we know what it wants?"

"It didn't say much," she replied. "It was angry, blamed me for what happened. Then it said I didn't know what I was talking about. It had a bit of a meltdown and threw the vase against the wall. That's what woke Jinx and I was afraid he was going to do something to hurt him. That's when I screamed."

Cooper was taken aback. "It threw a vase? I thought you said it wasn't corporeal."

Hannah took a moment to consider that. In the moment, when she'd first seen the demon, she didn't waste time wondering how it was suddenly so solid. That was a fact, though. The shadow from the night before was an actual being in her apartment … although it used magic to throw the vase. When she explained that to Cooper, his confusion only grew.

"Then how did it get out of the apartment?"

She shrugged. "I don't know. Maybe it can make itself corporeal at times. I can't answer that."

"Okay." He continued rocking, thoughtful. "Well, you're not staying here alone. In fact, I think maybe it would make sense to move into the extra room over the brothel until this is settled."

Hannah was flabbergasted. "You want me to stay in the brothel?"

Her reaction was enough to have him chuckling. "I'm not casting aspersions on your modesty, if that's what you're worried about. The demon has made it in here twice, though. I don't want to give him the opportunity for a third try."

That made sense in theory. Hannah had a few problems with the scenario, though. "What's to stop him from entering the brothel?"

"Nothing. Are you saying you want to stay here?"

"Well … ." She wasn't sure how to answer. "Not alone."

"And here we go." Tyler brightened considerably as he shifted and playfully smacked Cooper's arm. "And here you thought you were going to get shut out of the loving tonight. She just engraved an invitation for you."

Cooper didn't want to start yelling and frighten Hannah, but he was at his limit with his friend. "Tyler, I think it's time you headed down to your place. I'll take over watching Hannah for the rest of the night."

Tyler let loose a saucy wink. "You bet you will." He was feeling full of himself as he swaggered toward the door. "Do you want me to take Jinx so you guys can have proper alone time?"

Cooper was actually considering it, but only because Hannah seemed so worried about her furry friend. When she immediately started shaking her head, though, he thought better of it. She would never sleep if she was separated from Jinx.

"We'll keep Jinx with us," he insisted. "He'll be fine."

"Okay. Don't say I didn't make the offer, though, and don't come crying to me tomorrow if the dog ruins your play time."

Cooper managed to swallow a sigh, but just barely. "I will walk you out." He waited until he was in the hallway with Tyler to unleash his anger. "What is wrong with you? Do you really think now is the time to make juvenile statements like that?" Tyler was usually the sympathetic sort so Cooper had no idea why he was acting the way he was.

"Actually, I think now is the perfect time to say stuff like that," Tyler replied reasonably. "And, before you start screaming at me, keep in mind that's only going to make her feel worse. She's a bundle of nerves and she's exhausted. She needs sleep."

"And I'm going to make sure she gets it ... but not the way you're insinuating. I mean ... what sort of guy do you think I am?"

Tyler chuckled at his friend's outraged expression. "Don't clutch your pearls so tight, *Esmerelda*," he teased, grinning. "I know you're not the type of guy who would take advantage of a woman in this situation. Heck, I can't think of any situation where you would take advantage of someone. It has nothing to do with that.

"I want her to relax and laugh," he continued, not missing a beat. "She's coiled so tight she's bound to snap if you're not careful. I thought if I teased her, caused her to think of something else, she might ease up a little bit. I wasn't really trying to mess with you."

"Oh." Cooper had to admit that sounded like a good idea. "I guess I take back the mean things I said."

"You didn't say anything overly mean."

"I did in my head."

Tyler snickered. "I guess I had that coming. Honestly, though, I was trying to help her relax. I guess I'll leave the rest of that particular program to you."

"That would be best," Cooper agreed, peering down the stairs before resting his hand on the doorknob. "I need you to make sure the downstairs is locked up tight."

"I'll handle it. Also, don't worry about breakfast in the morning. I'll handle that, too."

"Can you call Boone and get him out here tomorrow morning? I think we all need to have a serious talk."

"I can also handle that ... and I agree. If that demon is hanging around out here, I'm honestly not sure we should open the town."

Cooper had been considering that himself. "Did you make the calls to the workers?"

"No. I was going to do that after I got my drink."

"Then hold off. Right now, I think it's best for everyone if we don't open tomorrow. That can't be the line we hold forever, but it's better to be safe than sorry. We just eradicated one threat in the form of Lindsey Lincoln. I don't want to risk someone else dying up here before we figure out exactly what's going on."

THROUGH A LOT OF CAJOLING — and some heavy cuddling — Cooper finally managed to lull Hannah to sleep. She slept in the middle of the bed, Jinx on one side and Cooper the other, and curled into him.

He held her the entire night, not relaxing until he was certain she slumbered without dreams chasing her, and even then he was on alert for the slightest noise in the apartment. Thankfully, for everybody, the demon didn't return.

After nine hours of sleep, Hannah finally stirred. When she opened her eyes, she found Cooper staring at her.

"Hey." She snapped awake, suddenly self-conscious. She'd forgotten she wasn't alone when she went to bed. "I ... you're still here."

He arched an eyebrow, amused. "Did you think I was going to slip away in the middle of the night? If so, I'm pretty sure I should be offended. That's not who I am."

She already knew that. "I didn't think you would or anything. I just thought ... maybe it was a dream."

Cooper understood what she was saying. "You were kind of hoping it was a dream."

"Not because of this," she said hurriedly. "I would prefer not seeing a demon, but this is really nice. I mean ... really nice. I wouldn't want to trade this."

"Just the demon stuff, right?"

"Yeah."

"I would trade that, too." He pressed a kiss to her forehead and then hunkered down a bit so they were at eye level. "This is definitely nice."

Hannah was certain her hair was a mess and she hadn't bothered to wash her face before turning in, despite the long soak in the tub. She probably looked a mess, but she didn't care. The way he looked at her said he didn't care either.

"What are we going to do today?" she asked when her heart stopped flipping.

He smiled, the expression lighting up his handsome features. "Well, I've been giving that some thought. Are you opposed to spending the entire day in bed?"

She shot him a churlish look. "I don't think we should be worrying about that when we have a demon on the loose."

"You've got a gutter mind, darling. I wasn't suggesting that. I thought we could spend the whole day in bed talking."

Instead of being charmed, as he expected, she snorted. "Oh, puh-leez." She rolled her eyes so hard it was a miracle she didn't tumble out of bed. "There's no way you and I are spending an entire day in bed together without something happening."

He grinned at her certainty. "I am a gentleman. I can control myself. You must be worried about your hormones taking over."

"Ha, ha, ha." She poked his side. She felt lighter than she expected and she was glad for his presence. "Your hormones are just as bad as my hormones."

"On the contrary. My hormones are polite and keep their hands to themselves."

"Good to know." She rested her chin on his chest. "I'm being serious, though. What are we going to do? A day in bed doesn't really seem like an option."

"It's not," he agreed, playing with the ends of her hair. It was long and wild after a crazy night, but it suited her. "Tyler is picking up breakfast. We should probably get cleaned up and head down. We're not opening Casper Creek today after all. I probably should've asked you before making the decision, but you had enough on your plate last night."

"I'm okay keeping the town closed another day. I don't want a demon attacking some poor, unsuspecting family."

"We're on the same page there. Boone is coming out and I asked for Jackie and the other coven members to be here. Basically we need to bounce ideas off one another and go from there because I'm completely out of my depth."

"Me, too." Hannah let loose a lengthy sigh. "Can we spend

five more minutes doing this? I know it's not an entire day, but I'm warm and cozy and not quite ready to get up."

As if agreeing, Jinx thumped his tail on the bed behind her, his eyes remaining screwed shut.

Cooper laughed at the dog's reaction. "How about ten minutes? We might as well milk it for as long as we can."

"That sounds like a great idea."

"Yeah." He nestled her close, his lips pressed against her forehead. "Once this is finished, though, I think we should definitely consider spending an entire day in bed together. I bet my hormones can outlast your hormones."

She laughed at the challenge. "You're on."

"Just so you know ... I like winning. I'll hold out on principle alone."

"That makes two of us."

"Now I'm really looking forward to it."

"That also makes two of us."

SIXTEEN

The group was already in the saloon when Cooper and Hannah hit the main floor. Jinx, apparently on a tear to get outside and greet the day, didn't take time to sniff anyone before bolting under the swinging doors and hitting Main Street.

"I take it he had some business to do," Tyler noted, grinning. "Did you guys keep him up all night with your ... *conversation?*"

Cooper shook his head and frowned. "I'm seriously going to beat the crap out of you later."

Tyler's smile never wavered. "I'm looking forward to you fitting me in your schedule."

"You're a big talker."

"I am. I can still take you."

Jackie made a tsk-ing sound with her tongue as she sat in a chair and graced both men with dark looks. She was in her sixties but looked ten years older given the way she glared. "I'm so glad I never had kids. I mean ... so glad."

Tyler winked at her. "You would love me as a son."

"That is a frightening thought."

"They're just arguing to make me feel better," Hannah announced, moving toward the makeshift buffet that Danielle was setting up. She was the resident cook at Casper Creek, but the food had been picked up at a neighborhood diner, which meant she made continuous faces as she glared at the takeout bags and fussed over the layout.

"Why would arguing make you feel better?" Jackie asked, confused.

"It's a guy thing. Last night they were afraid I was too morose so they started arguing to cheer me up. I think it's a *Three Stooges* thing."

Cooper pressed his lips together to keep from laughing. "I didn't think you realized what we were doing."

"You weren't doing it at first," she countered. "Tyler was the one doing it. Then you realized what he was doing and tried to join in. It was kind of cute ... and definitely sweet."

Cooper turned sheepish. "Well ... it's kind of embarrassing now that you know what we were doing."

"It's fine." She waved off his concern. "I needed the levity after ... well, everything."

"What's everything?" Boone queried as he strolled into the room. He looked well-rested, and yet troubled all the same.

"Actually, we were waiting for you to arrive so we could tell the story," Cooper replied. "We only want to tell it once."

"Speak for yourself," Tyler countered. "I plan on telling the story where I raced to a woman's rescue heedless of my own safety at least fifty times. I'm guessing it's going to get me applause."

Cooper pinned him with a murderous look. "She knows what we're doing so there's no reason to keep being ... well ... you."

Tyler snorted. "I'm always me."

"Knock it off," Boone warned, extending a finger to quiet

both men. "While I'm usually entertained by your antics, we have a lot going on and I don't think we should be focusing on this."

Cooper sobered. "You're right. What's going on?"

"Logan is locked up in a detention center for minors. Given what he's been accused of doing, they can't allow him to mingle with the other kids. That's probably a blessing in this particular case because he's the youngest one in the facility."

Hannah sank into a chair as she absorbed the news. "What are the odds of getting him out?"

"They're not good," Boone replied, opting for honesty. "They have pretty damning evidence, including eye witness testimony from two neighbors who saw him terrorizing the dog that went missing."

Sickness rolled through Hannah's stomach as she attempted to maintain her demeanor. "That is ... horrible."

"It is," Boone agreed. "It's definitely horrible ... and I don't see how there's anything we can do about it. The state police are handling the investigation. They're not going to believe anything I have to say once the word 'demon' comes out of my mouth."

"We have to try, though," Hannah persisted, refusing to give up. "He didn't do this. The creature inside of him is the guilty party."

Boone remained dubious. "Hannah, I don't want to crush your spirits, but there's very little I can do. You should be happy that you're off the hook. They're looking at Logan as a suspect in his father's death. I'm guessing they're looking for the same poison that killed the neighbor. Because of that, you're free and clear. Sure, Lindsey might try to sue you, but she'll be laughed out of court if she tries."

"I don't want her laughed out of court," Hannah countered. "I mean ... I don't want her to win or anything. I don't

169

want her to suffer more pain either. Believe it or not, I think there's something wrong with her, too."

Cooper slid her a sidelong look. "What do you mean by that?"

"Didn't you watch her yesterday?"

"You mean when she was threatening us for attacking her kid? Yeah, I watched her."

"That's not why she was threatening us. She was threatening us for invading her space. She was threatening us for money. She didn't care about Logan. Heck, she wouldn't even make eye contact with him."

Boone shifted, his gaze intense. "Wait ... go back. Tell me exactly what happened from the moment you entered the house until the moment we dragged Logan away. I didn't get a chance to question you yesterday. I want to hear all of it now."

"There's more than just what happened yesterday, too," Cooper interjected. "The demon we exorcised returned last night. It was in Hannah's apartment."

Jackie jerked up her head, surprised. "You're kidding. It's not dead?"

"No, but it's badly injured," Hannah replied. "He didn't attack me or anything. I'm okay. He was really angry, though, and he said I didn't know what I was talking about. He almost reminded me of a frustrated teacher or something. It was kind of odd."

"Demons lie," Becky volunteered, speaking for the first time. "They never tell the truth. That's part of who and what they are." She fell into silence for a moment and then continued speaking. "Is that why you were up there together? You didn't want to leave her alone in case she was afraid ... or the demon came back. I get it."

Hannah didn't miss the wistful way Becky stared at Cooper. It made her feel guilty, which was enough to make her feel angry, at herself. Becky was a nice enough woman, but she didn't owe her anything. Besides, Cooper hadn't shown as much as five seconds of interest in Becky. There was nothing to feel guilty about.

"I stayed with Hannah because we're together and we're going to be spending a lot of nights together," Cooper replied without hesitation, glaring when Tyler let loose a low wolf whistle. "I'm seriously going to kill you."

"Knock it off." Boone was like a cranky father as he rubbed his forehead. "I need you to tell me exactly what you saw. We'll deal with the demon after. Right now, I want to know what happened at the house."

Rather than questioning why Boone needed the information, Hannah launched into the tale. She wasn't afraid to add her stray observations to the mix. When she was done, Boone was even more pensive than when she started.

"What's wrong?" Cooper asked, his hand automatically moving to Hannah's back to soothe her. She seemed agitated after relating all the information to him.

"I don't know," Boone replied, rolling his neck. "I just ... things seem off. I don't know how else to describe it. Hannah's right, though, that's not the normal way for a mother to react. Why didn't she call for help right away? Why didn't she go to her child? I think we need to talk to her and Patrick again."

"Can we do that?" Cooper queried. "I would think the state police would shut off our access to them."

"Actually, it's the exact opposite. I told them we might need to follow-up for the investigation out here and they're more than happy to give us access to Lindsey and Patrick. Logan is another story. When I asked if we could talk to him they shut me down."

"He's a minor," Cooper pointed out. "There are different rules for minors and adults."

"There are," Boone agreed. "They were almost gleeful when they were shutting me down, though. It doesn't matter. Lindsey and Patrick are at their house and I'm allowed to talk to them."

"Maybe I should go with you to make sure all the questions get answered this time."

"That's a good idea."

Hannah stirred. "Maybe I should go with you, too."

Boone immediately started shaking his head. "Absolutely not. Lindsey is going to melt down if she sees you. We can't risk that. If we're going to get answers, it has to be Cooper and me. Even then I'm not sure she'll cooperate. She looked to be in shock yesterday."

"Maybe she'll be better today after everything has settled," Tyler suggested. "I mean ... it could work out."

"We won't know until we get there," Cooper replied. "I think we should have breakfast and then head out. After that, we need to come up with a plan to deal with the demon that keeps letting himself into Hannah's apartment. I'm not comfortable with that arrangement."

"I'm hitting the books right after breakfast," Jackie offered. "I thought for sure we killed him ... or at least scared him away. I can't for the life of me figure out why he would possibly come back."

"That makes two of us. I want answers, though. I don't like that Hannah is vulnerable in the one place she should always be safe."

"I'm on it," Jackie reassured him. "I'll figure it out."

"We'll all figure it out together," Boone corrected. "We're a unit and we won't stop until we've handled every stray detail. That's our only option.. It's going to be a long day."

PATRICK WAS THE ONE WHO opened the door when

Cooper and Boone came calling. He didn't look surprised in the least to see them.

"My mom is in the kitchen," he announced, stepping away from the door. "She's in a bad mood."

Cooper's heart went out to the boy. He was in an untenable situation. By all accounts, his father was a disagreeable man. He was prone to horrific outbursts and constantly yelled at his children. He was still his father, though.

Now his brother was sitting in a cell, charged with murder and other horrible acts of violence, and his mother was a morose mess. How much was the kid supposed to take?

"I'm sorry we have to bug you again," Boone offered, sincere. "We have some questions, though."

"You want to know about the thing inside my brother."

Boone swallowed hard and nodded. "We do. How long were you aware that there was something wrong with him?"

"There's always been something wrong with him." Patrick remained hovering in the hallway, seemingly afraid to lead Boone and Cooper to his mother. Because he was sympathetic, Boone allowed the boy to move at his own pace.

"What do you mean by that?" Cooper queried. "He must've been a normal kid at some point."

"No. He's never been normal."

Cooper assumed that was normal sibling rivalry speaking. "What about when he was a baby? I'm sure he was annoying, crying all the time and stealing your parents' attention, but that's fairly normal."

"He didn't cry."

Boone was taken aback. "Never?"

"No. Not that I remember at least. He was a quiet baby. That's what my mother always said. She expected him to be more like me. If you believe her, all I ever did was cry and make things hard for her."

If Cooper didn't already dislike the boy's mother, he would've switched his opinion based on that comment alone. "I don't understand," he said finally. "Babies cry. That's what they do."

"Not Logan. He never cried as a baby. When he got older and started school, he never cried then either. When adults ordered him to take a nap, he didn't do it. He did lie down and stare at the ceiling for hours, though. He was always up at night, but he learned to keep quiet while running around so as not to tick off Dad."

Slowly, Boone slid his eyes to Cooper. He was legitimately confused. "Did your mother ever get him tested?"

"Tested for what?" The new voice was decidedly female and Cooper cringed when he turned to the hallway on the opposite side of the room and found Lindsey watching them.

"Tested for any neurological or psychiatric problems," Boone continued, not missing a beat. He didn't look surprised at Lindsey's sudden arrival. The way he flicked his eyes toward her drink — which looked to be bourbon on the rocks — told Cooper there would be trouble before the visit was over.

"There is nothing wrong with Logan," she snapped. "He's a normal boy. I know what you guys are thinking but none of the things he's accused of are true. You're just trying to cover up for your blond friend on the mountain. You're trying to protect her."

"Hannah didn't do anything wrong," Cooper shot back. "She's a good person."

"You mean you're hot to trot for her." Lindsey sipped her drink, her narrowed eyes bouncing between faces. "Why are you even here? You've won, by the way. I don't have the money to fight what you're throwing at me. My attorney says winning a civil suit against your girlfriend is going to be difficult anyway."

"You're still going to try, though, right?" Cooper challenged.

Lindsey shrugged, noncommittal. "I haven't decided yet. My husband is dead. Someone should have to pay for that."

"I believe your son is going to pay for that," Boone pointed out. "He's the one we want to talk about."

Frustration clouded Lindsey's already twisted features. "Logan is a good boy. He's not capable of doing the things they're saying. I mean ... he's ten. He's a child."

"That's what we want to talk to you about." Boone chose his words carefully. "We're trying to ascertain when it was that Logan changed. It might be helpful for his court case if we can pinpoint what was happening in his life when he started acting out."

"That's what I'm telling you," Lindsey spat. "He doesn't act out. He's never acted out. I mean ... if you look up the term 'perfect child' in the dictionary, you find his face."

Cooper immediately started shaking his head, annoyance bubbling up. "You don't believe that. The kid might not have found regular trouble, but that doesn't mean he was an angel in human clothing. I'm willing to bet the opposite." Expectantly, he turned his gaze to Patrick. "You said he never cried. It sounds like he never slept either. Was it always like that? He must've slept as a baby."

"What have you been telling them, Patrick?" Lindsey's voice was tinged with accusatory distaste. "You shouldn't even be talking to them."

"They asked," Patrick replied. "Besides ... I want to help them. They're the ones who helped me."

"I'm your mother. All I've ever done is help you."

"No, Mom, that's not true." Patrick gripped his hands into fists at his sides, his temper on full display. "You always put Logan ahead of me ... and Dad. You never saw the truth about either of them."

"And what truth should I have seen?" Lindsey protested. "Your father was a good man, a good provider. Our lives are going to be much worse without him."

"Dad might've been a good provider, which basically means he went to work on time every day and did his job, but he wasn't a good father. He yelled at us all the time. He threatened us. You should've heard the things he said to Logan. Oh, who am I kidding? You heard. You just ignored everything he said because you were lazy."

Lindsey's eyes flashed. "You take that back. Your father was a good man."

"He was a jerk."

Boone held up his hand before Lindsey could explode and unleash a pile of vitriol on her son. "I want to hear what he has to say."

"It's all lies."

"I don't happen to believe that." Boone gestured toward the couch. "Patrick, I know this is difficult for you, but I want to hear everything you can tell me about your father ... and your brother."

"See, this is just about them trying to get more dirt on Logan," Lindsey hissed. "We're not going to allow that. We're not going to tell you anything."

"What do you want to know?" Patrick asked, legitimately curious. "My dad wasn't a good guy. He was mean to Logan all the time, to the point where I felt sorry for Logan ... and that wasn't easy to do because Logan was evil, too."

Cooper cleared his throat to get the boy's attention. "You must have stories about your brother. We want to hear them."

"Which ones?"

"Any that stand out in your head. We're especially interested in when he changed, or at least when you noticed there was something wrong with him. It could be important down the line."

"How?" Lindsey asked, suspicious. "How is any of this important now? It's already over."

"Logan is in a home, not prison," Boone countered. "He's a minor. They're not going to put him in prison with hardened adults. They'll keep him in a home until he's eighteen, maybe even twenty-one. After that ... there are a variety of things that could happen. Logan's life doesn't have to be over."

"We need information, though," Cooper insisted. "The more information, the better. We need everything you can give us."

Patrick let out a sigh and nodded. "Okay, but remember, you asked for it. I have a lot of stories."

"And we want to hear all of them."

SEVENTEEN

*S*ince Jackie, Becky, and Danielle were busy doing research — something Hannah felt she was ill-equipped to help with — she decided to take Jinx for a walk. The dog was antsy after the exploits of the previous night and eager to hit the great outdoors.

To Hannah's surprise, Becky followed her out.

"Is something wrong?" Hannah asked when she realized the woman was trailing her.

"No." Becky shook her head, unsure. "It's just ... are you and Cooper really dating?"

In hindsight, Hannah realized she should've expected the question. Becky's crush on Cooper was obvious ... and a little sad. Still, now was not the time for this conversation. "Perhaps you should ask him that," she suggested. "It would be best if you waited until after we dealt with the demon."

Becky frowned. "I'm not trying to be difficult."

"I didn't say you were."

"But you're acting as if it's a ridiculous question."

Hannah sighed. Apparently they were having this conversation after all. "I don't know what you want me to say," she said finally, internally debating about which tack she wanted to take. "I get that you think you have feelings for Cooper."

"I don't think," Becky shot back, cutting Hannah off with a brutal glare. "I've known Cooper a long time. I've been here for years. I used to have a summer job in Casper Creek when I was a teenager. Did you know that?"

Hannah shook her head. "I didn't."

"I spent a lot of time with your grandmother, something you can't claim."

Irritation, sharp and hard, punched Hannah in the stomach. "I didn't get a chance to know my grandmother," she snapped. "There were things ... things that happened. I was kept away from her. I would give anything to be able to fix that, but I can't."

Perhaps sensing that she'd overstepped her bounds, Becky held up her hands to soften her previous comments. "I didn't mean to jump all over you like that. I understand that you didn't really have a choice in the matter with Abigail. I don't know why I said that."

Hannah had a few guesses. "You're upset that Cooper spent the night with me." It was a statement, not a question.

"It's just ... I've always felt this pull toward him." Suddenly, Becky looked like a vulnerable young woman struggling under the weight of emotions she couldn't understand. "When he was dating Astra, I knew they wouldn't last. It was like she was a temporary placeholder or something.

"It's not that I stalked them or anything," she continued. "I don't want you to think that. I watched them, though, and neither one of them seemed that ... enamored ... with one another. They spent time together, but they both had other things that were more important."

Hannah felt caught. "I don't understand why you're telling me this."

"Because he's not that way with you." Becky suddenly

turned pitiful. "He listens when you talk. He's always watching you, even when you're not saying anything. He's hyper-aware of how you react to things."

"And you don't like that," Hannah surmised.

"I don't," Becky agreed without hesitation. "If you guys actually get involved I don't think there's ever going to be room in his life for anybody else."

"Meaning you don't think you'll ever get the chance with him you feel as if you deserve."

"You probably think I'm a selfish wretch." Becky was rueful. "If our positions were reversed, I would want to beat the crap out of you. I know you think it's just a crush, but it's more than that."

Hannah tilted her head, considering. In truth, she was more convinced than ever that what Becky felt for Cooper was a crush. The girl couldn't see it because youth obscured her vision. Eventually she would realize that she was acting like an idiot. Until then, though, she would continue to obsess about a man that was never going to feel the same way about her as she felt about him.

"Listen, I don't want to demean what you're feeling," she started, grasping for the correct thing to say and coming up short. "You should probably talk to Cooper about this, though. It doesn't have anything to do with me."

Becky frowned. "I can't talk to him about this. It's embarrassing."

"Trust me. He already knows." It was a haphazard comment but the way Becky's face flooded with color told Hannah she'd said the exact wrong thing. "I just mean that ... um ... well ... ."

"What do you mean he already knows?" Becky grew unnaturally pale. "How is that possible?"

Hannah opted for the truth. "You're not exactly subtle with the comments and digs. It's obvious you dislike me ...

and why. Now, I'll admit that men don't always catch on to these types of things, but Cooper isn't an idiot. He sees what's going on and he struggles with it because he's a good guy."

"You're assuming that he's going to shut me down. You don't know that. He might be open to the suggestion."

To Hannah's mind, Becky was acting delusional. She didn't want to point that out, though. "You should do what you think is right. I'm not the person to discuss this with, though. You need to talk to Cooper."

"Well ... maybe I will."

"I think that's best for everybody."

Becky narrowed her eyes. "You're pretty smug, huh? You just assume that Cooper is going to choose you even when he knows all the facts."

In truth, Hannah was convinced Cooper had made his choice long before he spent the night. She didn't have time for petty conversations, though. There were other things to worry about. "Talk to Cooper," she prodded. "I think that's going to be best for everybody."

"Oh, I'm definitely going to talk to Cooper. You can count on it."

COOPER AND BOONE SAT IN WINGBACK CHAIRS across from Patrick and Lindsey. The latter kept rolling her eyes and making huffing noises. The former, however, seemed lost in thought.

"I don't know where to begin," the boy nervously stated, gripping his hands together on his lap. "There's so much to say ... and some of it might sound weird."

"I work in a town where people pretend to be from the Old West," Cooper reminded him with a smile. "I'm familiar with weird."

"Yeah." Patrick spared a glance at his mother, who looked to be having some sort of inner conversation with herself that wasn't going well. "Like I said, he was a weird baby. I know I'm only two years older than him, but I remember being about five or so — which would've made him three — and I found him sitting in the sandbox in the backyard. He was ripping worms apart and laughing."

Boone frowned as he shifted. "As gruesome as that is, I think that's a boy thing. He might not have realized he was destroying something."

"I guess, but that was hardly the first time he killed stuff just for the fun of it. He went after bugs all the time when he was really little. Then, when he was five or so, he started going after squirrels and birds."

Lindsey stirred. "What do you mean by that? How could he go after them?"

"He threw rocks ... and set traps. I don't know how he figured out the traps. They were weird. He took netting and rope from the yard and he would trap squirrels ... and chipmunks ... and birds. Whatever he could get his hands on."

"And he killed them?" Boone queried.

"Yeah. He liked it. He would bash their heads in with rocks. Sometimes he would cut them open with a knife."

At this, Lindsey scoffed. "What knife? We got rid of all the knives in the house when he was four and threatened to kill your grandmother by slitting her throat."

Boone cocked an eyebrow, dumbfounded. "And you didn't think it was weird for your four-year-old to threaten to kill his grandmother?"

Lindsey balked. She clearly didn't like taking the blame. "Um ... excuse me, but little kids do that all the time. Patrick used to pretend he was the Hulk and threaten to smash everything in the room."

"That's normal," Cooper noted. "The Hulk is a superhero

... and saying things like that and following through are entirely different things. I'm willing to bet that Patrick has never killed an animal."

Patrick swallowed hard. "You would be wrong there, sir."

Cooper was taken aback as Lindsey's eyes filled with triumph.

"See!" She jabbed a finger in his direction. "I told you Logan was normal. You think he's a monster, but he's a normal boy."

"He's not normal," Patrick countered. "He's pretty freaking far from normal. I only killed a rabbit — it was actually a small bunny — because he was torturing it and I didn't want it to suffer."

Boone took pity on the boy and nodded in understanding. "You did what you had to do. When was it that Logan killed the bunny?"

"He was seven."

Lindsey started vehemently shaking her head. "No. That's not right. I think I would know if my son was torturing animals. There's no way he could hide it."

"He didn't hide it," Patrick countered. "Dad knew. Dad buried all the animals. Dad told me not to say anything. Dad is half the reason this went on for as long as it did."

Lindsey opened her mouth, something acidic on the tip of her tongue, but Boone cleared his throat and sent her a warning look before she could unleash whatever fury she had building in her son's direction.

"When did your father first find out what your brother was up to?" he asked after a beat. "I mean ... when did he find out about the animals?"

"I don't know." Patrick shrugged. "I remember him finding a dead squirrel when Logan was about four. He thought a neighborhood cat ripped it apart. I wanted to tell him then that it was Logan, but I was afraid.

"After that, more animals turned up and Dad figured it out at some point," he continued. "He was furious and yelled at me. He thought I was doing it. I said it wasn't me and he didn't believe me at first ... but then he started watching Logan."

"Watching him how?" Cooper prodded. "I mean ... did he say anything to your brother?"

"He said things to him a few times, but Logan wasn't afraid. You know how most kids are afraid of their parents?"

Boone shook his head. "Actually, no. Children should never be afraid of their parents. That's not normal."

"Maybe afraid isn't the right word," Patrick hedged. "I never wanted my Dad to be disappointed. That always kind of made me freeze up. Logan didn't care about that. It was almost as if he was playing games with Dad."

"Can you give us some examples?"

"Well ... Dad had dirty magazines in his shed that he liked to look at." Patrick shot his mother a worried look, but her face remained placid. If the magazines were a surprise, she didn't show it. If she was upset about the revelation, she was holding it back. "He would go out there and look at them sometimes.

"We knew about them because we stumbled across them when we were looking for wood to build a treehouse one day," he continued. "Logan wouldn't stop looking at the magazines. I mean ... I looked at them, too, but that's all Logan wanted to look at."

"I think certain magazines are a rite of passage," Cooper offered, uncomfortable. "I don't know that looking at the magazines means anything."

"It wasn't just looking at the magazines. Sometimes he would rip pictures out. When Dad realized what was happening, he totally flipped out. He started yelling and screaming. He threatened to take our bikes away. He wanted to know which one of us ripped apart his magazine."

"Did you tell him?" Cooper asked.

"I was afraid to." Patrick was sheepish. "I was looking at the magazines, too."

"What about Logan?" Boone pressed. "Did he own up to mangling the magazines?"

"He didn't say anything. He just let Dad melt down. After that, Dad started hiding the magazines. Logan turned it into a game to find them. Each time he did, he trashed the magazine even more."

"How so?"

"He started drawing on the photos. Um ... he used a red pen to look like blood and made a lot of the women look dead. Dad was really mad and he ended up burning all the magazines. I asked him why and he said he didn't want proof around the house in case Logan did something. I wasn't sure what that meant, but I figured it wasn't good."

Boone and Cooper exchanged heavy looks.

"At some point your father figured out it was Logan, right?" Boone finally asked.

Patrick nodded. "He was different after that. Between the animals and the magazines ... he seemed sadder. He and Mom started fighting all the time. I heard him telling her there was something wrong with Logan, but she always argued against that."

Boone's gaze was accusatory when he turned it on Lindsey. "You managed to leave out that little tidbit, huh?"

She merely shrugged. "I don't know what you want me to tell you. My husband was prone to dramatic fits. You want me to agree with what Patrick is saying, but I can't. Logan is a good boy."

"Who you can't look in the eye," Cooper pointed out. "You're afraid of him, too. I don't know why you won't admit it. He's locked up now. He can't hurt you." Something occurred to the security guru and caused him to square his shoulders. "Did he ever hurt you, Mrs. Lincoln?"

"Absolutely not." Lindsey was fervent as she shook her head. "He's a good boy. He's always been a good boy."

"He never hurt her physically," Patrick volunteered, drawing attention back to himself. "He liked playing different sorts of games with different people. Like Old Mr. Peterson on the corner? He's always complaining about us riding our bikes on his lawn because the sidewalk is rough over there and it's killing the grass. Once Logan figured out that he could drive Mr. Peterson crazy, he started stealing weed killer from all the neighbors and dumping it in spots on Mr. Peterson's lawn."

"Let me guess." Cooper intoned. "Mr. Peterson is one of those people who really cares about how his lawn looks, right? It's a status symbol for him."

"I don't know about the status symbol thing, but he brags about having the best lawn in the neighborhood," Patrick replied. "Logan pretty much destroyed Mr. Peterson's yard for fun."

"Oh, this is preposterous." Lindsey threw her hands in the air. "The yard thing was funny. It's not as if he was committing mass murder of grass blades. It was just a joke."

Cooper found her admission interesting. "I'm guessing you knew more about your son's exploits than you've been letting on."

"He was just playing games," Lindsey sputtered. "All kids play games."

"Your son's games were deadly, though," Boone pointed out. "He's a suspect in his own father's death. You can't be so blind that you don't realize exactly what you're up against here."

"He's a child," Lindsey snapped. "They won't put him in prison. They can't."

"I agree that they can't put him in prison." Boone was solemn. "If they did, he would be a nightmare to protect from the other inmates given his size. The thing is, we came here because we're trying to ascertain when Logan changed. That might sound odd, but it's important. What Patrick is telling us is that he's always been like this. That doesn't make a lot of sense to us."

Cooper had been trying to figure out the exact same thing. "Do we think the demon was with him from birth? I didn't know that was possible."

"Demon?" Lindsey sat up straighter on the couch. "What are you people even talking about? This is just ... I can't even ... this is too much." She slapped her hands over her eyes. "I can't believe this is even happening. I need another drink."

"You need to pull yourself together and take care of the son you have left," Boone barked, wrinkling his forehead when the cell phone in his pocket started ringing. "I apologize. I have to take this, though. One second."

Cooper watched his friend with curiosity as he answered the call. Boone fell silent as he listened to whatever the voice on the other end of the line told him. Finally, Boone spoke again, his tone clipped.

"I'll head out to Casper Creek to be on the safe side," he stated. "I think odds are long that he'll head that way, but it's probably best to at least look around. I'll let you know the status of my search when I get out there."

Cooper found his body had tensed as he waited for Boone to disconnect. The sheriff immediately got to his feet, telling Cooper something had gone very, very wrong.

"Is it Hannah?" Cooper asked, fear coursing through him. "Did something happen to her?"

Boone shook his head. "No, it's not Hannah. At least I don't think it is."

He looked pained, which set Cooper's teeth on edge. "What is going on?"

"There's no easy way to say this, so I'm just going to say it. That was the state police. It seems there was an incident at the hospital Logan was sent to for observation last night."

"What kind of incident?"

"A security guard is dead and Logan is missing. It seems he's escaped. Every police organization in the county is now looking for him."

Cooper was dumbfounded. "But ... how is that possible? We exorcised the demon."

"I don't know how it's possible. The state boys are worried he's going to head back out to Casper Creek. That seems like a legit possibility, although it would be smarter for him to run. I'm just not sure he's that smart."

"He's not," Patrick volunteered. "If he thinks your group is a threat, he'll go after you just for fun. He likes torturing people."

Cooper's heart skipped a beat. "Hannah. He pegged her as his main adversary. We have to get back to her."

Boone nodded grimly. "Then that's what we'll do. We need to head out. I think waiting is a very bad idea."

Cooper was in full agreement.

EIGHTEEN

*H*annah still had Becky's declaration running through her head when she left Casper Creek. Jinx was happy with the walk and yipped in excitement as he checked out every bush. In the back of her mind, Hannah worried about another rattlesnake showing up, but she managed to tamp down the fear. Cooper said it was rare for the snakes to be in the area where Logan was almost attacked. She hoped the odds were against it happening twice in the same week.

It wasn't a conscious decision — or maybe it was and she simply didn't want to admit it — but she pointed herself toward the creek. If Astra was going to show, share information, it would have to be at the creek because they'd essentially cut off her access to the town.

Hannah hummed to herself as she snapped her fingers to get Jinx's attention. The dog had shifted from fixating on the bushes to staring at a spot underneath a large tree. The dog was so focused, in fact, Hannah slowed her pace and watched him for signs of distress. She assumed he was looking at an animal, but the more she stared, the more she managed to make out a faint outline.

"Abigail?" She wasn't sure it was her grandmother's ghost. It was a feeling more than anything else. Her gut instinct was rewarded. Her grandmother's form solidified.

"It's me." She almost looked relieved. "I've been trying to contact you for days."

Hannah furrowed her brow as she stepped closer to the ghost. "I don't understand. Why didn't you just come to the apartment?"

"I tried. It hasn't been ... easy."

If Hannah didn't know better, she would've guessed the specter was in pain. She was fairly certain that wasn't possible, though. "Is something wrong?"

"Something is very definitely wrong," she agreed. "You need to cross the creek."

Hannah was taken aback. "I don't understand. Why would I do that? Cooper says that's a bad idea."

"Cooper is a sweet boy who has a heart of gold. Your safety is important to him, which I respect and admire. He's not here, though, and Astra needs help."

Hannah licked her lips, uncertain. She trusted her grandmother. Sure, she was a ghost, but she seemed to be a friendly ghost. Still, something about this scenario felt wrong. "Did she send you?"

"I know what you're thinking."

"I don't think you can possibly know what I'm thinking."

"Let me take a shot. You're worried that Astra has somehow been keeping me from you, that she might be controlling me. You don't trust her, which is wise. That's not what's happening, though.

"I've been having trouble controlling my new reality, which I've explained to you," she continued. "It takes more effort than I thought it would. It's frustrating. That's not why

I've been AWOL, though. Something did keep me away. It wasn't Astra."

Something occurred to Hannah. "Was it the demon?"

"It was definitely a demon, although not like you're imagining. I don't have time to explain things to you. The demon's energy has been dwarfing mine. Once I'm stronger, that won't be an issue. That's not a discussion for today, though. Astra is in trouble and you need to get to her."

"Would she do the same for me in similar circumstances?"

"No. You're not her, though."

Hannah wanted to argue. Her brain told her this was a bad idea. Abigail's plaintive expression had her following her heart. "Okay, but if this is a set-up and she tries to kill me, I'm never going to let you forget it. I'm going to haunt you for the rest of your days."

Abigail managed a wan smile. "That sounds exactly like something I would say under the same circumstances."

"Lead the way."

"You need to hurry. I'm not sure how much time I have."

BOONE AND COOPER LANDED IN Casper Creek with minimum fanfare. There weren't a lot of workers on the premises so Cooper started calling for all of them when he hit Main Street.

"What's wrong?" Tyler asked as he scurried to greet his friend. "Did something happen?"

"I don't know." Cooper opted for honesty. "We've been talking to Patrick and Lindsey Lincoln. The mother is in denial. Patrick had some interesting — and, quite frankly, very disturbing — information."

"What is that supposed to mean?"

"He says that Logan was troubled from the start," Boone

volunteered. "If a demon really did possess him, it did it at a young age."

"Hannah saw the demon, though," Jackie pointed out, her expression grave. "Something was definitely in that boy and we forced out the presence."

"I understand that." Boone was matter-of-fact. "That doesn't change the fact that the kid has been demented from the time he started walking. He's been messing with his parents ... and other kids in the neighborhood ... and even older adults since long before he should've even been able to grasp what was going on."

"What does that mean?" Becky's expression reflected confusion. She'd purposely picked a spot close to Cooper because she was determined to make her feelings known before the day was out. He might not be interested, might still choose Hannah, but she wanted him to have all the information.

"We don't know," Boone replied. "There are multiple possibilities. The kid might be a sociopath. That could be why it was so easy for the demon to get a foothold in him. There might've been nothing inside, nothing good at least, to keep out the demon. It might be something else entirely, though."

"Like what?" Becky remained baffled. "What sort of creature takes over a small child?"

"We don't know that anything took him over back then. He might just be evil."

"Why don't you talk to him?" Danielle queried. "That makes the most sense to me. He's going to have the answers you want. Can't you get in to see him?"

"Actually, we can't but that's not the reason we're here. I got a call when we were at the Lincoln house. Logan has escaped from the hospital."

Jackie immediately started shaking her head. "I'm sure we exorcised the demon yesterday."

"I'm sure you did, too. That doesn't change the fact that Logan managed to escape ... and he killed a guard before slipping out. I'm starting to think the demon wasn't the issue."

"Or maybe the demon made him twice as bad as he normally would've been," Cooper suggested. "Maybe he was evil, the demon stumbled across him and saw an opportunity, and together they were two or three times as evil as they would've been without one another."

"I guess." Jackie didn't look convinced. "That means we have two problems, though. The boy is missing. If you're up here, that must mean you think there's a possibility he's up here, too. We know the demon is up here because he's approached Hannah twice."

Cooper shifted from one foot to the other, an idea popping to the forefront of his brain. "What if they both came up here because they want to reunite?"

Boone shot him a keen look. "That would take a level of planning I'm not comfortable with."

"Me either. I'm not sure they planned it, though. Maybe they can feel each other, are drawn together."

"Then that would mean they're weaker apart," Tyler said pragmatically. "We need to hunt them down when they're separated."

"And then what?" Becky questioned. "Are you suggesting we kill that boy? That's not going to go over well with the authorities. They're not going to believe us when we claim it was necessary because he was evil."

"She has a point," Boone conceded. "We can't kill the boy. We can kill the demon and take the boy back into custody. I think that's the best outcome we can hope for."

"So we'll aim for that." Cooper lifted his head and scanned

the street. "Where is Hannah? I thought she would come down when she heard me calling."

"She took Jinx for a walk," Tyler answered, grim. "They looked to be heading toward the creek."

"Son of a ... ." Cooper viciously swore under his breath.

Boone reassured him, resting a hand on his shoulder. "We'll all head out and find her. If we're lucky, she'll have already tracked down the demon for us."

To Cooper, that sounded extremely unlucky, but he managed to keep his opinion to himself. He had other things to worry about. "We'll break into teams," he announced, making up his mind on the spot. "One man and one woman. Once we find her — or Logan and the demon — we'll text a location and regroup. If we can, we need to try to take them on as a team. I know that might not be possible given the circumstances, but we have to try."

"Then we'll try," Tyler said. "Try not to worry. We'll find her."

"We're definitely going to find her," Cooper agreed. "Then, once we do, I'm going to kill her."

HANNAH WAS FOCUSED ON KEEPING her footing even as she followed Abigail's ghost over a rocky incline. She had no idea where her dearly-departed grandmother was leading her but there was no turning back at this point.

"How much farther?"

"Soon," Abigail replied, taking a moment to stare at Hannah's flushed face. Even though Hannah tried leaving Jinx at the bottom of the craggy rock formation, the dog insisted on following. His tongue lolled out of his mouth and he didn't look particularly agitated. Abigail had no doubt that would change once they reached their destination.

"Perhaps you should try to tie Jinx in the shade somewhere," she suggested, absently looking around. "The climb is only going to get more difficult."

Hannah had already considered that before ruling it out. "No. If something happens to me, he'll die out here. I won't do that to him."

"A fall could hurt him, too."

"Do you think I don't know that?" Hannah's eyes flashed with irritation as she regarded her grandmother. "You're the one asking a favor of me. If you're going to keep this up, I can turn around and take Jinx back to town. Is that what you want?"

Abigail planted her ghostly hands on her ethereal hips. "Now you listen here, Missy. I'm your grandmother. I know you didn't grow up knowing me. I'm sorry for that. I still deserve a modicum of respect."

Hannah worked her jaw. "Fine. I respect you. I don't need constant reminders about Jinx, though. I can't tie him up. The thought of him dying of thirst or hunger — a slow death — kills me. I don't like worrying about him being injured either. The only thing I can do is stick with him. Besides, if I tie him up, he'll kill himself to get loose. I'm not going to just leave him behind."

Abigail let loose a weary sigh. "I get what you're saying. You love the dog."

"You have no idea how much I love him. He's the one thing I brought from my old life. There's a reason for that. He was the only good thing I had."

Sympathy rolled over Abigail's features. "I'm sorry you were so miserable."

"You shouldn't be. I did it to myself."

"I don't believe that. You're a good girl. Things are going to get better for you here. I promise you that."

Oddly enough, Hannah believed her. "We should keep going. If Astra is really in trouble, we need to get to her."

"She's definitely in trouble," Abigail agreed. "Also ... we're there. She's right inside."

Confused, Hannah furrowed her brow and glanced around. As far as she could tell, they were in the middle of nowhere. Then, as if a fog suddenly cleared, her gaze fell on what looked to be an opening between the rocks.

"Oh, geez." She made a face. "Are you going to make me go inside of a cave?"

Abigail was rueful. "You're not claustrophobic, are you?"

"Not really. I mean, I don't love enclosed spaces, but I don't freak out or anything. Dark and dank places that are probably filled with snakes are a different story, though."

"Can you do this?"

Hannah held her grandmother's gaze for an extended beat and then nodded. There was no turning around now. "Yeah."

"Then let's do this."

BECKY MANAGED TO WRANGLE Cooper as a partner and she was flush with glee as they headed toward the creek.

"It's a beautiful day."

Cooper merely grunted in response. All he could think about was Hannah ... and getting to her. Everything else was superfluous.

"I'm glad we got a chance to spend some time together," Becky offered. She had to struggle to keep up with him — his legs were much longer than hers — and her breath was ragged as she worked to maintain her pace. "Maybe we can go out to dinner or something once this is all over."

"I think I'll be busy killing Hannah tonight. She's not going to want dinner when I'm done with her."

"Yeah, but ... I'm talking about you and me having dinner," she stressed. "Hannah wasn't invited."

Cooper didn't slow his pace, but the look he shot Becky was incredulous. "You have to be joking."

"Why would I be joking? I think a private dinner, just the two of us, is something we would both enjoy."

Cooper wasn't always observant when it came to women. He didn't pick up on certain nuances without help. He was well aware of Becky's crush on him, however. He hoped it was something she would outgrow. Perhaps she would meet somebody else, he often thought. Actually, he fervently hoped for it. The fact that she was choosing now to move on this situation was beyond frustrating. He didn't want to hurt her, but he had to nip this conversational topic in the bud ... and right quick.

"Becky ... ."

Perhaps sensing that he was about to shut her down, she kept talking so he would have no choice but to keep quiet. "We have a lot in common if you really think about it. We both love the outdoors. We're both familiar with the area. We both love Old West stories. You can't say the same about Hannah."

"Hannah and I have different things in common," he said after a beat, causing her to frown. "I don't think now is the time for this conversation. Hannah could be in real trouble."

"If she is, she caused it herself," Becky barked. "And what do you have in common? She's from the city. You always said you liked the country. I heard you talking to Tyler one day. He asked what sort of woman you wanted. He was being serious.

"You said you wanted someone easygoing, who loved the outdoors and was perfectly happy spending an entire afternoon just sitting in a field and staring at the sky," she continued, barely taking a breath. "That's me. We're perfect for each other."

Cooper would've preferred being somewhere else. Really,

anywhere else would do. Hannah needed him, though. He could feel that in his gut. He didn't have time for this conversation.

"I'm not attracted to you." Cooper knew it was brutal to lay it out that way, but he didn't have a choice. Becky had to let this go. "I'm sorry if that hurts your feelings, but it's the truth. We don't have any chemistry."

Becky made a protesting sound with her tongue. "That's not true. I feel tons of chemistry whenever we're around one another."

"Well, I don't."

"But—"

"No." He held up his hand, firm. "You honestly couldn't have picked a worse time for this conversation. I was hoping you would find someone else who was more age-appropriate at some point, but I didn't get that lucky."

Becky balked. "You're not that much older than me."

"Maybe not in years, but in life experience I'm an octogenarian. You're still a child in that respect. We really have nothing in common. Like ... absolutely nothing."

"That's not true. You're blind to how cool I am because of her." Becky knew she sounded bitter, but she couldn't stop herself. "All you care about is Hannah. I think she cast a spell on you or something. There's no other explanation."

"She did cast a spell on me," he confirmed, not backing down. "It's just not the kind of spell you think. From the moment I saw her, I was attracted to her. We have chemistry. She has life experience that's not exactly similar to me, but she's lived. More importantly, she's loved and lost. She's also learned. You haven't done any of those things."

"Then you could teach me." Becky knew that she was coming across as desperate, but she couldn't stop herself. "We could do it as a team."

Cooper felt sorry for her, but he didn't have time to

soothe her frayed feelings. "I'm already a team with Hannah. I know you don't want to hear it, but we fit … and I'm not backing away from her. It's simply not going to happen."

"She said that you'd say that." Becky's lower lip quivered, making her appear even younger than her twenty-three years. "She said that you would shoot me down. I wanted to kill her when she said it, but she was right."

"When did she say that?"

"Before she left on her walk. She told me to talk to you about my feelings when I asked her to stay away from you."

Frustration bubbled up in Cooper's stomach. It tasted like acid. "I can't believe you actually asked that of her. That is just … ridiculous."

"I have a right to feel what I feel."

"And I have a right to feel what I feel," Cooper shot back. "I want to be with Hannah. I think I've wanted to be with her before I even met her — and, yes, I know that sounds ridiculous — but things simply fit with us.

"Now, I'm sorry if your feelings are bruised, but I can't help that," he continued. "None of this matters right now. Hannah is in trouble. We have to find her. I'm not stopping. I'm done with this conversation. You can either stick with me or go. I really don't care.

"The only thing I care about right now is finding Hannah." His eyes flashed with determination. "You can stay or go. I'm done worrying about stupid crap, though. What you do with the rest of your day is up to you."

With those words he put his head down and increased his pace. There was a warning sounding in his head … and it told him Hannah was in big trouble. He had to get to her. He was already out of time.

NINETEEN

*H*annah wanted to take back her declaration that she wasn't claustrophobic the second she entered the cave. She had to duck her head to slip through the opening, but the corridor widened about twenty feet inside. That was the only bit of good news she had going for her.

"I hate this." Her voice cracked with emotion as she reached out a hand to touch the cool stone wall. "I really want to turn around."

"You can't." Abigail was insistent. "Things will get better once you're around that far corner."

Hannah had her doubts, but she sucked up her fear and kept walking. "They had better. If I don't like what I see around that corner, though, I'm leaving. You've been warned."

Instead of being offended, Abigail chuckled. "I bet you were fun as a kid."

"If you believe my father, I was actually an easy kid. He tells a few stories that make me think otherwise."

"Parents always remember things differently from kids.

What you might've thought was the end of the world in your youth, he probably wrote off as a youthful indiscretion."

"Yeah, well ... I—" Whatever Hannah was going to say died on her lips. Once she turned the corner, all the oxygen escaped from her lungs. There was so much to register in a short amount of time she didn't even know where to start.

"Hello, Hannah," Astra drawled grimly. She sat in the middle of the cave floor, two lanterns hanging from branches jutting out of the cave walls offering limited illumination, and she was cradling her ankle as she glared at a dark figure in the corner.

Slowly, even though she didn't want to acknowledge the trouble she was about to be facing, Hannah tracked her eyes in that direction. There, fury etched over drawn features, stood the demon who invaded her apartment the night before. He looked weak — as if he might fall over at any moment — and he curled his lip and began snarling when Jinx began barking.

"Why did you bring that hateful beast with you again?" the demon complained. "I'm going to make him shut up if you don't. I swear it. I'll enjoy it, too."

Hannah turned an accusatory set of eyes to Abigail. "You tricked me."

Abigail immediately started shaking her head. "I swear I didn't. I was watching Astra for other reasons when she hurt herself. I wasn't sure she would offer you the information you needed. She's not always the most reliable witch."

"Thanks," Astra said dryly, making a face. "I can't tell you how much that means to me."

"Oh, don't give me grief." Abigail rolled her eyes. "You're lucky I got help in the first place. After everything you've done—"

"Yeah, yeah, yeah." Astra turned a set of plaintive eyes to

Hannah. "Thanks for coming. We seem to have a situation, though."

Hannah had figured that out for herself. "I see that." She shifted from one foot to the other as she regarded the petulant demon. "What did he do to you?"

"What did I do to her?" The demon was incredulous. "What makes you think I did anything to her? Have you ever considered that she invaded my space and attacked me? Of course you didn't. You just hear the word 'demon' and naturally assume that means I'm an awful individual. I'll have you know that I'm not. I help people. I used to run an animal rescue in the last body I inhabited."

Hannah rolled her eyes. "You're afraid of my dog, who is the biggest lover on the planet. There's no way you ran an animal rescue."

"It was for ferrets. They're far superior to dogs."

"In what universe?"

"In every universe."

Astra cleared her throat to end the argument. "Um ... can we talk about something else? It's not that I'm not fascinated with the dogs-versus-ferrets argument, but I'm in pain and I want out of this cave. I'm going to need help to do it."

Hannah shifted a wary eye to the demon. "I'm assuming he won't let you go."

"Oh, there you go again." The demon's expression twisted. "Way to make assumptions. I'll have you know that I want her out of here as much as she wants to leave. She invaded my space. I was minding my own business when she came in here and started jabbering away. I didn't hurt her, by the way. She was so surprised when she saw me that she tripped."

"That's true," Astra acknowledged. "He's kept his distance. I think it's because he's afraid of me."

The demon snorted. "Oh, that is priceless. I just can't even ... ." He shook his head. "Get your friend out of here and leave me to die in peace. I'm sick of you people. I don't want to spend my last hours with you."

Hannah took a tentative step in Astra's direction and then stilled. Something about the situation didn't feel right. Er, well, other than the obvious. "I don't understand," she said finally, opting to push the conversation as far as she could. "You're allowing me to take her out of here. That's what you're saying, right?"

"That's what I'm saying." The demon sagged against the cave wall. "I just want to die in peace."

Hannah risked a glance at Astra and found the woman watching the demon with the same intense reaction as she felt.

"Why don't you want to kill us?" Astra asked finally. "I mean … you're a demon. You should want to kill us."

"You're a human. Do you want to kill everybody because other humans do it?"

Astra nodded. "A lot of the time."

Hannah shot her a dark look. "Don't listen to her. She's not a normal human being. In fact, I'm not even sure she really is human."

"Oh, that's rich," Astra snapped. "I'm the one who was injured doing research for you in the first place and now you're attacking me. That's just … see if I ever help you again."

Hannah was more confused than ever. "You were doing research for me? In a cave? That doesn't make any sense."

"I wasn't doing research in here. I was looking for river rocks. There used to be some in this cave. How do I know? Because I stored them in here."

"River rocks? Why would that be important?"

"Because they can be used to kill my kind," the demon replied, eyes heavy. "I was looking for them myself to end things quicker. That's why I'm in here."

"Oh, well … ." Torn, Hannah made up her mind on the spot and moved closer to the demon. "Can you show me where you're hurt?"

Astra was incredulous. "Are you kidding me? You're going to help the demon instead of me. This is just … ." Her eyes flashed with annoyance when they landed on Abigail's ghost. "This is all your fault. I told you that Casper Creek should've been mine. She's so stupid she's going to ruin everything."

"Shut up, Astra," Abigail intoned. "I don't want to hear another word come from your mouth."

"Right back at you."

Hannah ignored the squabbling and extended her hands as she stepped forward. "I just want to see," she promised the demon. "I don't want to hurt you."

"I believe you've already hurt me," he shot back. "You're the reason I'm in this mess. Well, you and the other witches who ripped me from the devil boy."

Hannah swished her lips but continued forward, stopping when she was directly in front of the demon and lowering herself to a knee. Her fingers were shaky, tentative, as she reached out. Instead of putting up a fight, though, the demon let loose a dramatic sigh and leaned so she could see the wound better.

She almost wished he would've kept it hidden. The huge, gaping hole in the creature's side was oozing and gross, to the point where she was certain she would have nightmares. She swallowed hard.

"Well, that doesn't look good," she said finally.

"Oh, you think?" The demon rolled his eyes. "Can't you just kill me and get it over with? I'm ready to leave this world."

"I'll kill you if someone will carry me over there," Astra offered. "Just so you know, I'm going to collect all your bile first, though, because it's useful for potions and spells."

"Ugh. Make that thing shut up." The demon sounded weak and pathetic. "I need to die. Why can't I just die?"

The more the demon talked, the more confused Hannah got. "How did this happen?" She gestured toward the wound. "I mean … this almost looks as if someone ripped part of your body apart and then … took it or something."

The demon heaved out a dramatic sigh. "That's basically what happened."

"And we did this?" She felt guilty, which was odd given the circumstances. "I thought we were basically blowing your consciousness out of Logan. I didn't realize we were tearing you apart."

"You did blow me out of his body," the demon confirmed. "You have no idea how excited I was when you guys showed up. I knew exactly what you had planned. I thought I would finally be able to carry out my escape."

"Your escape?"

"From the boy."

"I don't … ." Hannah flicked her eyes to Astra, unsure. "Do you know what he's saying?"

"A little," Astra confirmed. "We had a talk while we were waiting for you."

"Wait … you knew I was coming?"

"Abigail said she would get help," Astra clarified, her white hair gleaming thanks to the limited light allotted from the lanterns. "I thought she meant Cooper. When she came back with you, I was disappointed but … beggars can't be choosers, right?"

Hannah was doing her best to keep from exploding, but she was starting to consider the fact that it might be a lost cause. "Just so I'm clear, you thought Cooper was going to rush to your rescue. While you were waiting, however, you had a talk with the demon. Did he explain anything of importance?"

"Just that it was the boy providing the evil influence," Astra replied. "He says that the boy sought him out. He's corporeal when he's outside of the boy – although he can change that up because he's a shadow walker – and loses his form inside."

Hannah wrinkled her nose. "How does that work?"

"It's a modern marvel," the demon drawled. "What does it matter how it works? Basically I was minding my own business, fostering ferrets, and that little … heathen … called me to him. I wasn't even sure what was happening. Do you know the last time I was forced to possess someone? No? I don't either because it's never happened."

Hannah was truly at a loss. "You're saying that Logan called you to him because … why?"

"Because he wanted my magic. Demons have powers, too. Witches aren't the only ones with magic. I know you guys like to feel high and mighty, but it's simply not true."

"I know very little about witches," Hannah admitted. "I know even less about demons. I'm trying to understand, not torture you or anything. I'm simply confused. You're basically saying that a small child somehow called you to him and then trapped you inside so he could use your magic to do terrible things."

"If I had opposable thumbs, this is where I would flash one in your direction," the demon drawled. "You nut-shelled it, but that's basically it."

Hannah rolled the new information through her head. "What is Logan?"

"That's a good question." Astra perked up. "If he was strong enough to trap you, that means he has to be something good."

"He's a Cambion. His father was a demon that mated with a human. He must've been a powerful demon to create that little monster."

"Todd Lincoln was a demon?" Hannah queried. "That doesn't sound right. How did he get caught unaware if he knew what his son was?"

"Todd Lincoln wasn't the boy's father," the demon countered. "The mother had an affair. Todd knew it. That's why he treated the boy so terribly. He blamed the boy for existing even though the mother was clearly seduced. If I had to guess, it was an incubus ... and a powerful one. I can't be sure, though."

"Oh, that makes sense." Astra shifted on the floor. "I've always wanted to meet an incubus. I think we would have loads in common."

"Since you're both evil?" Hannah shot back, rolling her neck. "I've read a little on incubi. Just basic stuff. They seduce and conquer, right? I thought they killed with sex."

"That's often the case," the demon confirmed. "Apparently he didn't kill Lindsey, though. Todd knew the boy wasn't his, but they stayed together. Things probably would've been better for all concerned if they separated.

"Todd was incredibly cruel to Logan – something I witnessed on a regular basis – but Logan treated it like a game," he continued. "He trapped me inside of him, tapped into my magic, and went on a neighborhood mayhem spree.

"He killed dogs and cats ... and neighbors. Some neighbors bothered him enough that he thought death was too easy and he tortured them in other ways. Like Sandra Clarke. She tattled on him to Lindsey numerous times, got his video games taken away, so he used my powers to influence her husband to cheat on her ... and then announce the information at a neighborhood barbecue in front of everybody. He got off watching her fall apart."

Hannah was officially horrified. "So, when we blew you out of the boy, he tried to keep hold of you and that's how you were injured."

"Pretty much."

"Can you be healed?"

"Yes, but I would need to visit the healing springs. I can't as long as the boy holds me here."

"Holds you here?" Hannah straightened. "How is he doing that?"

"He's powerful. We have a bond now thanks to the fact that we've shared a body for so long. He can find me whenever he wants … and he's coming."

Hannah's blood ran cold at the prospect. "He's coming out here? Why? How will he be able to find this cave?"

"I sensed the cave when he was out here the other day. I could smell the river rocks. They were gone, but I could smell the remnants. I thought if I could overtake him long enough to find the rocks that I would be able to kill myself. Even death is better than being caught in that devil's mind. You have no idea."

Things slowly started to slip into place for Hannah. "Did you charm the snake?"

The demon nodded. "The boy and I were fighting for control that day. When I sensed the snake, I thought I had an out. If the snake bit the boy, his human body would've failed. Eventually, once he grew weak enough, I would've been able to escape. You stopped that when you froze the snake."

"Good job," Astra enthused, sarcasm practically dripping from her tongue. "That was a smart move."

Hannah balked. "I didn't know. How could I possibly have known that?"

"You couldn't have known," the demon replied. "I don't blame you for this. That's why I didn't kill you, even when I had the chance. I did try to warn you the night I entered your apartment in my shadow form. When I returned, I was simply looking for healing springs ointment. I sensed you had some in the apartment. I was not trying to hurt you."

Hannah slid her eyes to Abigail. "Is there healing ointment in the cabinet?"

Abigail nodded. "Yes. Have you managed to open it yet?"

"The other night."

Abigail clapped her ethereal hands, although no sound came out. "That must mean you opened your heart to Cooper. That's the only way the key would've appeared. You had to make a real connection with him."

Astra's mouth dropped open. "Are you serious? That's what happened to the key? You magically cloaked it so she could only get it if she hooked up with Cooper?"

"Don't be ridiculous." Abigail turned prim and proper. "I wanted her to let go of the past and make a connection for her future. Cooper was not specifically part of the spell. The fact that he was a key in his own right is simply a coincidence."

"Let's not talk about that because it upsets my stomach," Hannah suggested, returning to a standing position. "The important thing is that there's ointment in the apartment. I'm guessing that will be enough to keep you alive, right?" She waited for the demon to nod. "I need to get it."

"You need to get me out of this cave," Astra countered. "Screw the demon."

"I'm going to get you out of the cave, too," Hannah promised. "I can't carry you, though. I'm going to need help. That means I need to run back to Casper Creek, get the ointment and Cooper, and then come back. It shouldn't take me more than forty-five minutes."

Astra's eyes narrowed and Hannah was certain she was going to say something obnoxious. She didn't get the chance, though. Shuffling on the rock floor, signifying a new presence in the cave, was enough to snag her attention.

When Hannah looked to the opening, she expected to find help in the form of Cooper or Boone. Heck, maybe even

Tyler. Instead, her blood ran cold when she realized it wasn't the cavalry arriving. It was something else.

"Well, this is just … neat," Logan intoned as he took in the multitude of faces. "I can't believe you all lined up this way for me. I really appreciate it, though. You have no idea."

TWENTY

"*A*nd I thought things couldn't get worse," Astra announced, dissolving into a series of ridiculous giggles. "I just … this must be the little devil himself. Logan, right? I'm so glad to meet you."

For his part, Logan looked less than impressed. "I don't care about you," he said after looking her up and down. "You have nothing to offer me."

Despite the surreal situation, Astra had the gumption to be offended. "Hey! I could offer you a great deal. If you get me out of this cave, maybe we can strike up a bargain."

"No." He waved his hand in Astra's direction, causing her to go suddenly mute. When she realized she wasn't making any noise, she grabbed at her throat. Logan was clearly over talking to her, though, because his attention had drifted to Hannah. "You, on the other hand, are more interesting. I wouldn't mind getting a look inside your head."

Hannah ran her tongue over her teeth, unsure how she should respond. When she shifted her eyes to the spot Abigail had been floating in only moments before, she found the space empty. The realization that she was on her own didn't sit well. "I'm kind of using my head right now. Maybe another time."

The demon barked out an amused laugh. "Oh, you're funny. Too bad you hadn't realized what was going on earlier, huh? I bet you wish you would've let that snake bite him now, don't you?"

Honestly, Hannah was getting to that place. She felt like an idiot for not realizing the true nature of the boy before this. Now was not the time to dwell on it, though. She couldn't go back in time and change things.

"You really did mess up there," Logan noted. "You have no idea how hard our friend worked to get me into that situation. I was frozen, couldn't move. I would've surely died thanks to that snake if you hadn't intervened. I owe you."

"In that case … why don't you let us all go?" Hannah suggested. "That can be my payment for services rendered."

"I can't have that." Logan made a scolding sound with his tongue. "You also screwed me by stealing my demon. I'm here to take him back. You have no idea how hard it was to escape from that hospital with nothing but my size and some latent magic to help me. I much prefer being more … proactive."

He talked beyond his years, Hannah noted. He was an adult – an evil one at that – trapped in a child's body. Life had to be difficult for him. That didn't excuse the things he'd done. Also, the fact that he was clearly here to commit murder didn't help his cause either. Still, Hannah felt as if she should at least try to talk to him.

"You don't have to do this," she supplied. "You can't absorb the demon into you again. He won't survive."

"You should let him absorb me," the demon countered. "If he does, he'll die with me."

Logan frowned. "I think you're making that up."

"Try me on for size," the demon suggested. "I might be dying, but I'll gladly take you with me."

Logan's expression turned so dark Hannah was convinced he was about to lapse into a rage. She wasn't wrong. "This is all your fault," he hissed, his eyes flashing red as he glared at the blond witch. "You tried to steal my demon from me. You caused this."

"If you'd just let him go instead of digging your claws into him, this wouldn't have happened," Hannah argued. "You really have no one to blame but yourself."

"Oh, I can blame you, too." Logan took a menacing step in her direction. He was clearly done playing around.

Hannah expected him to move on her. She was prepared. Well, at least as prepared as she could manage given her location and lack of skills.

She lashed out with a bolt of magic. She had no idea if it would hurt him. She honestly just wanted to slow him down. The magical torrent caught him off guard because he let loose a terrific growl.

On a whim, Hannah threw out a huge gust of wind. It was strong enough to kill the lights in the lanterns. She remembered the layout of the cave well enough that she managed to sidestep the boy as he fruitlessly searched for her and landed next to Astra.

"We have to move," she hissed. "We don't have time to screw around."

Astra still couldn't talk, but Hannah could feel her bobbing her head in the darkness. Hannah gripped the woman under her arms and tugged her to a standing position, dragging her toward the opening in the cave. They'd moved a good ten feet before the lanterns flared to life again.

"Oh, that was pretty good, witch," Logan sneered from behind them. "You almost had me. It's been a long time since I was frightened of the dark, though. You're out of time."

Hannah risked a glance over her shoulder and found the boy was dangerously close. Thankfully, she hadn't just killed the lights when she unleashed her magic. She'd done a little something else, too.

"I think you're the one out of time," she replied, her voice low. "You really shouldn't have reminded me of the snake."

"Oh, no? Why is that?"

Hannah inclined her chin. "Because these caves are full of snakes."

Realizing too late what Hannah was insinuating, Logan turned at the exact moment the snake by his left heel struck. The demon was controlling the snake. It was obvious by the way his face twisted in concentration.

Logan yelled out when the snake's fangs sank into the soft skin above his shoe. Hannah took advantage of his distraction to drag Astra through the opening. She stopped long enough to stare at the demon. He didn't move even as more snakes slithered out from various hiding places. Instead, he watched the scene with grim satisfaction.

"I'll be back for you," she offered quickly. "I'll bring the tonic. Hopefully that will be enough to get you on your feet so you can go to those springs you mentioned."

The demon nodded, weary. "I won't last much longer. If you're really going to do it, make it soon."

"I'll be back," Hannah promised. "The snakes won't bite you, will they?"

"Even if they did, I'm immune. Don't worry about me. Get out. You don't want to see the end anyway."

Logan swatted at the snakes as they encroached on his space, letting loose a pitiful mewling sound.

No, Hannah decided. She definitely didn't want to be there for the end.

. . .

COOPER AND BECKY MET THEM AT the mouth of the cave. Cooper swooped in so fast Hannah thought she might fall over when he pulled her in for a hug. Astra rolled her eyes and made a series of groaning noises, which only got worse when Cooper helped her to the ground.

"Abigail found us by the creek," he explained. "She told us where to go."

"That's good." Hannah was relieved her grandmother hadn't merely run when the going got tough. Still, there were other things to worry about. "Logan is in the cave. He's been bitten by at least one rattlesnake. I wouldn't be surprised if it's more at this point. We could still get him to the hospital."

Cooper studied her for a long beat. Her discomfort was obvious. He understood what she was thinking. On one hand, he was a child. It seemed wrong to let him die in a cave. On the other, he was responsible for multiple deaths and would always be a threat – to them and others – if they saved him.

"I'll check on him," he said finally. "Maybe we'll get lucky and the decision will be taken from us."

"Wait." Hannah grabbed his arm, stilling him. "There are snakes everywhere. You probably shouldn't go in."

He held her gaze, uncertain. "Are you sure you want to make that call?"

"Yeah," she nodded. "I'm going to run back to Casper Creek. There's a tonic I need for the demon."

Cooper's eyebrows winged up. "So … now we're saving demons?"

"He's not so bad. He rescues ferrets in his free time."

Cooper exhaled heavily. "Do what you gotta do."

That was exactly what Hannah intended all along.

LATER THAT NIGHT, COOPER let himself into Hannah's

215

apartment. He had a bag full of takeout Mexican in one hand and a six-pack of Corona in the other. Hannah was expecting him so she wasn't surprised when she exited the bathroom in her fuzzy robe and found him doling out the food.

"That didn't take you long." She greeted him with a shy smile. Her hair was soaking wet and her face devoid of makeup. She felt exposed. The way Cooper looked at her, however, told her he didn't care about either of those things.

"Boone met me at the Mexican place," Cooper explained, pulling out a chair so Hannah could sit at the table. "Just for the record, the official story should the state police come snooping around is that we never saw Logan."

Hannah's stomach constricted. "We're going to lie?"

"Do you think telling the truth is somehow better?"

"Actually, I do," she confirmed, taking him by surprise. "I don't think we should do it right away. I think we should wait a few weeks and then someone should accidentally stumble across his body in the cave."

"Why do you think that's better? I'm not saying it's not, but I'm curious why you want to handle things that way."

"A few reasons. For one, once Logan is found, the state police will have no reason to hang out up here. For another, once he's laid to rest, Patrick won't have reason to be afraid that his little brother is going to show up one day and kill him."

"Ah." Cooper bobbed his head. He'd filled Hannah in on what Patrick told them while waiting for Boone to show up at the cave. It made sense she would worry about the boy left behind. "I guess that makes sense. This way, Lindsey won't always wonder what happened to her son either. She'll know."

"She probably won't care," Hannah said. "She'll know, though."

"We'll arrange for his body to be discovered in a week or

216

two," Cooper promised. "Your demon friend should be on the mend and gone by then. He promised not to hang around and he's heading for some hot springs one state over as soon as he's strong enough to travel."

"He has ferrets to take care of."

"No matter how many times you say that, it's not going to make me like him any better. I would've been fine with him dying, too."

"I wouldn't have been okay with that."

"Which is why you helped him and I'm not going to give you too much grief over it." Cooper flashed a charming smile as he handed her a takeout container. "I had them withhold the onions, just FYI."

"Why? I love onions."

"Because I have plans for you that onions are going to infringe upon."

Hannah's cheeks flooded with color. "Oh, well … ."

He chuckled at her shy smile. "Not those sort of plans. At least not yet. I just want to kiss you senseless … all night."

"All night, huh?" A wicked grin lit Hannah's face. "I guess I can live with that. What happens tomorrow, though?"

"Tomorrow is another day. The town will open again. We'll go back to work. In twenty-four hours, the worst thing we'll have to worry about is the other workers giving us grief for dating."

"Are you worried about that?"

"Nope. Are you?"

She tilted her head, considering, and then shook it. "I don't really care what anyone else thinks. I just care what you think."

"I'm right there with you." He leaned close and briefly pressed his forehead to hers. "I'm looking forward to the adventure."

"Me, too."

He gave her a soft kiss and then pulled back. "Now you know why I held off on the onions. You can thank me later."

"I just might do that."

"Oh, you're definitely going to thank me. Trust me. I've thought ahead."

"I guess we'll have to wait and see."

Made in the USA
Monee, IL
07 May 2023

33257472R00132